The Mosaic IX
A Compilation of Short Stories

EDITED BY DR. C. WHITE-ELLIOTT

This book contains works of both non-fiction and fiction. In the cases of fictional writings, the stories may have been fashioned after true stories but are not exact retellings.

CLF Publishing, LLC.
www.clfpublishing.org
909.315.3161

Cover design by Senir Design. Contact information: info@senirdesign.com.

ISBN # 978-1-945102-56-1

Printed in the United States of America.

Dedications

This book is dedicated to all aspiring writers who were told they couldn't make it in the field of writing or who may have been too scared to move forward because of a fear of failure.

The writers, whose stories are included within, are proof that you can be successful and your dreams can be a reality.

So, I invite you to pursue your own writing and be the success you know you are.

Dr. Cassundra White-Elliott

Acknowledgements

I acknowledge all the participants in this project, who helped to see it from its stages of inception to its complete fruition.

May your success be plentiful, as you continue to pursue your educational and writing endeavors. I look forward to working with each of you individually, collectively, or both, in the near future.

Much love and appreciation,
Dr. Cassundra White-Elliott

Table of Contents

Introduction

Welcome to **The Mosaic IX**, where you will enter the exciting world of short stories. Here, the imagination can and will unfold right before your very eyes. What you least expect just may become the expected.

The authors have delved within their own imaginations and pulled out all the stops and barred no holds. Their tales will excite you, cause curiosity to grow, bring tears of sadness, and/or even feelings of wonderment.

They are skillful in their craft, and they are to be congratulated for their efforts. Most of them have stepped into unknown territory with publishing to share their talents with the world at large.

Also, included in this edition of the Mosaic are sneak peaks of full-length novels. A chapter from each has been included for your enjoyment. If you enjoy the chapter so much that you want more, details on how to obtain the full novel is listed at the end of the chapter. All of the authors appreciate your support.

So, I invite you to sit back, relax with your favorite drink, curl up in your most comfortable chair and be prepared for the journeys that lie ahead.

Edited by Dr. C. White-Elliott

With no further ado, I invite you to ENJOY!!!!!!!!!!

"As iron sharpens iron,

So a man sharpens the countenance of his friend."

Proverbs 27:17

64th Street

There was an uneasy feeling inside as I sat on the bathroom sink, looking into the mirror, into my own eyes. I was only three years old, but I knew there was something else to this living thing. As I sat there, just staring, I don't know if it was a voice or a thought, but it said I would not live. It said, eventually, I would die. Tears started to roll down my face as I sat there, just staring. The feeling became so overwhelming that the tears started flowing uncontrollably, and I started to sob. *What am I made for? How did I get here? What's after death?*

I guess my mother heard me crying and came to the bathroom. "What's wrong with you?" she asked, with a puzzled look on her face, holding the telephone receiver to her ear.

"I don't want to die!" I cried.

"Shut up, boy!" she said, as she slapped me and pulled me down off the sink. "Get your butt out of here!"

It was 1979, in South Central Los Angeles. 64th Street was our place of residence: my dad, my mom, my big brother Joseph Jr., and me. My dad was renting a one-bedroom apartment from his sister Briana and her husband Paul. Dad had a good job working for the city, but for some reason or another, we didn't have much. Joseph Jr. and I shared a fold-up rollaway bed that we slept on at opposite ends. That was the living room's only piece of furniture. Mama often complained to Dad that he should buy a couch and a coffee table at least, to make it feel like a home.

"This is not how I was raised, Joseph!" she cried. "What do you do with your paycheck? Just wait until I find me a job! You're going to see a change around here!"

"Shut up, woman!" Dad exploded. "You don't know what you're talking about! We don't need all that extra stuff!"

And, on and on they would argue until Dad would run out of words. Then, his hands started doing the talking. I'd be standing outside the closed bedroom door with Joseph Jr. calling for Mama, but the yelling and the crying would continue until it just died down. Sometimes, we would fall asleep by the door, tired from crying. Mama called the police a few times on the next day when she was released from her captivity and Dad was gone to work, but the cops said it was a domestic dispute, and they needed to straighten it out between themselves.

The violence continued...

One day, Mama taught Joseph Jr. how to dial 911, so he could save her from Daddy. "When you hear me crying, what are you going to do?" she asked.

"Call 911!" shouted Joseph Jr.

"That's right!" she said.

Mama took Joseph Jr. through a whole training course! She took him outside, so he could see the address of the apartment. She even walked him to the corner, so he could memorize the street signs. I wonder if she knew I was learning too, by just watching my brother go through boot camp. I was as sharp as a knife even though I was a year and a half younger. I had been learning my ABCs and 123s in little Joseph's preschool class while my mother volunteered. We were ready! Despite the fact that it was very confusing to be in between a war going on with two parties we both loved dearly, it seemed natural to be enlisted in Mama's army because we spent the majority of our time and training under her supervision.

"Ray! Ray! Raymond, put those marbles up, and let's go!" my mother shouted across the room.

"Oh, okay, Mama," I said as I filled my pail with Joseph Jr.'s and my marbles. Sometimes, we could play with those marbles for hours, but then it would be time to take a walk through the neighborhood to the local grocery store. My mother would speak to every neighbor as we went, and sometimes, they would visit for hours, talking about who knows what. It seemed as though she knew everybody! That could be a long trip depending on who was outside. "Looking good, Rachel," said Cleophus, with his chin on his chest.

"Ain't you supposed to be working?" Mama snapped with a smile still on her face.

"Check this out, I can fix these cars with my eyes closed and still have time to peek at you," Cleophus smirked.

"Leave me alone. I told you I was taken, oil man," Mama flirted.

"Is that whom you put that perfume on for?" Cleophus asked. Mama just continued to push the stroller past the auto body shop with that schoolgirl smile on her face. The grocery store was coming into view. I had my mind on those Neapolitan candies Mama usually gets for us as a treat, but Mama had something else in mind. In fact, she didn't go to shop for groceries at all. As soon as we entered the store, she immediately walked up to one of the women cashiers.

"Excuse me. I'm not trying to be rude, but I have something important to talk to you about," my mother said with a calm voice.

"Well, I don't get a break until another hour," proclaimed the cashier as if she was talking to the manager, who was twenty feet away.

"Okay, well here it goes," Mama reached into her purse and pulled out a small piece of paper. "My name is Rachel. You've seen me here before with my husband Joseph Watkins. I found your number in a pair of his pants, Sarah!" Mama said sternly, as she put the piece of paper next to the cashier's nametag. "I'm letting you know that he is married, and these are his two boys. If you have any decency that your parents raised you with, you will not continue to break up my family. You have a nice day," Mama said sarcastically, as she pushed me out of the store with Joseph Jr. trying to keep up with his little legs as he held onto the stroller. The cashier lady just watched us leave with her mouth open, a little embarrassed. I was wondering what happened to the Neapolitan candies, but I dared not ask and become the scapegoat onto which Mama's anger was released.

Being the granddaughter of a gospel preacher, Mama handled the situation quite well. It seemed that a humble spirit was seeping in, which unfortunately, had skipped her father. Her dad was a man whom neither Joseph nor I ever got to meet. Granddaddy Raymond, named after his dad and whose name I shared also, was a stern man, who was always spoken of as having a boiling hot, bad temper. He had gotten into an altercation with a young man when Mama was just a little girl.

The young man had owed two dollars to Granddaddy Raymond that he borrowed at the corner store. Granddad had obviously lost his patience while waiting for the two dollars to be paid back to him and went to confront the young man about it. Having the temper that he had, the conversation elevated into a fight, which, in turn, elevated into a stabbing. When the smoke cleared, Granddad had lost his life. Some say he died over two dollars, but anyone with any street smarts would say that the young man did not keep his word.

*****YOU HAVE JUST READ CHAPTER 1 OF

LET ME TELL YOU HOW I GOT SAVED,

A NOVEL BY CHARLES LEWIS ANTHONY*****

*****TO READ THE COMPLETE NOVEL, YOU CAN PURCHASE A COPY AT
BARNESANDNOBLE.COM OR AMAZON.COM*****

Born in the 1970's and raised in the 1980's in the gang-populated city of Los Angeles, California, Ray Watkins had to make some decisions for himself. Some turned out bad, and some turned out good, but the important thing was to stay alive and live to see another day!

Sit back as Ray takes us on a journey of street life survival and his encounter with our Heavenly Father.

CLF Publishing, LLC.
www.clfpublishing.org

ISBN 978-1-945102-29-5
90000

9 781945 102295

Charles Lewis Anthony's books are available at:
www.creativemindsbookstore.com
www.amazon.com
www.barnesandnoble.com

The Drifter

Christopher Ball

Truth is so obscure in these times, and falsehood so established, that, unless we love the truth, we cannot know it.

- Blaise Pascal

A spaceship orbits just outside the solar system of a binary star. If you could even call it a ship, it looks beat up with pieces of it that seemed to be scavenged from many other different spacecrafts, parts of which looked to be jerry-rigged to work with the older model in which they are placed on. The ship just hovers there, looking out at the twin stars, one bigger than the other. Around them there are clouds of gas and dust with many asteroid belts, but, of course, you can't see most of this with the naked eye.

"It started here, the war, I mean. These fields of asteroids, dust, and heat. At least, that's where the information has led me."

This person, in a drab very well-worn space suit and cloak, rotates a holo cube in his hand; he looks lost in thought, remembering the long adventure he had finding this treasure as the blue cube reflects its dull light off the visor of his helmet. Certainly, the scorched and pitted armor plating of his suit can attest to it many times over.

"But, is it really here? The evidence of what I'm seeking. What was it that put us to near extinction? All that we have, all that we have ever known is by what was told to us deep down from history and it . . . is vague."

He switches on the ship's sensors. Within moments, a 3D map of the solar system displays in front of him on the dashboard of his control panel. Closely, he examines all the details of the solar system.

As he expands the clouded areas of dust and gas, he finds a half blown apart planet.

"Alund'ar."

Putting away the holo cube, he turns on the thrusters of his spacecraft and plots his ship's course trajectory.

"There will finally be answers."

The ship boosts away rapidly into the blackness.

The ramp of the rugged ship slams down onto dead ground. Plated boots pound down to the surface. The drifter looks out across the empty plane of a dead world. He looks down at the device in his hand then looks up and proceeds straight from his position.

All around him are large jagged rocky pieces of land jutting up from the surface and many canyons, some unnatural in look as if something huge made them, of which the fall would be infinite. All this land iced over creating many sharp surfaces. It's so dark here, barely any light reaches through but what does casts long strange shadows in amidst the shaded land. In the sky is a huge planet, half of it missing. As it rotates, a hole can clearly be seen straight through it.

After some time, he stops before a huge structure. With the light from his helmet, he peers into the massive doorway. Besides the ice, what can clearly be seen are pillars and way in the back . . . "Something is glowing."

Entering the large room, he cautiously moves forward. Passing the pillars that are three times wide as he is tall. Proceeding down the steps, there can be seen a light emitting atop a pedestal. All around are numberless skeletal remains piled on top of one another, bleached white in their ashen remains. Closely, he looks and finally makes out something strange. A sword. A sword pierced straight through an obsidian tablet. The intense glow is being emitted from the sword, and it is so bright that it is hard to even tell at first that the tablet is even black. The drifter walks closer, up the pile of bones, to stand before the pedestal.

"Nothing was mentioned of this. Swords haven't been used since primitive times."

Cautiously, he reaches for the sword's hilt. Just before he is about to grab, it a sharp voice pierces his mind.

"STOP!"

Pulling his hand back quickly, the drifter looks around. Nothing. The room is empty.

~ Who was that? ~

Again, the drifter tries reaching for the sword. Just as he is about to grab ahold of its hilt, a hand of glowing white grabs his arm stopping him. Surprised, the drifter darts his head right to see a man in a white robe with every bit of him glowing. An angel?

"Son of man, remove yourself from this place."

"Who are you?"

"I am a part of the promise sent from who your surviving people call the Great Creator. My duty is to guard this place."

The angel lets go of his arm, and it falls to the man's side.

"The Great Creator failed us, His people. He was supposed to be there to protect us. We were nearly wiped out, and we lost our friends the Elves. They're dead. They are all dead! HE was not there for us."

There was a pause in the angel, not out of fright or anger but of solemnness. This angel was many feet taller than he was, but he spoke softly saying,

"The moment this darkness was released, we were waiting. When the galaxy was mostly covered by its blackness, we were sent, by Him. For, we saw Man and Elf losing in great numbers to the darkness. We fought this evil by your side without your knowledge. When they reached your home worlds, most of the evil was destroyed throughout the galaxy. What was witnessed at that last battle was a small portion to the sliver that was left. Man and Elf prevailed. Be it at great cost."

As the angel told these words, the drifter's mind was given a vision of all that the Great Creator had done in defense of His people. Waves of blackness and metal crashing against armies of angels. The darkness was scary, but the angels of light were easily taking down the evil with every stroke. In the end, no angels had fallen, nor a robe even torn.

"Why didn't we witness you defending us?"

"It was wisdom in the Great Creator that we should not be seen for Faith is still needed."

The man looked to the sword that was driven into the obsidian tablet.

"What about this? Why is it here, and what is it?"

"This is the heart of darkness. That sword keeps it still. It is kept as a reminder of its evil. Soon, it will leave this place to be destroyed, but there is purpose here, and so it stays, for now."

About the Author

Christopher Ball was born in Redlands, California. He grew up in the mountains of San Bernardino in a little town called Crestline. He now resides in Utah where he is finishing his schooling at Weber State. Chris likes video games, tabletop Warhammer 40k, puzzles, card games, gun sports, manga, painting, and anything else that is fun. He also has one little bunny, which he takes care of with his sister. If you want to message him about his created works, you can reach him at Christopher2013ball@gmail.com.

Sunshine's Quest for the Lost Feather

Michelle Ball

"Even in the darkest of storms; the sun is always shining!"

Anonymous

We have all heard of the Easter Bunny, but none has heard of the time of how the Easter Bunny directly brought Spring to the land or even how he came to be. This is one of many stories of how Easter came to be, and it takes place in a little town called Springville. This is just a small, little warren. Nothing special about it at all.

All the little bunnies of this warren live happy and carefree, as all bunnies do, knowing only good things. And it is all thanks to the special gift of the phoenix father who had compassion upon the little bunnies and decided to give them one of his feathers. With this feather, the bunnies were no longer able to live in fear of their lives. Now, they run and jump and play all day, and they have a good clean land to farm their food and make clothing and other items.

In Springville, every bunny was happy; and Sunshine was the happiest of them all, even though she was considered a bound bunny by her society. This is one who has not yet received a calling due to her talents, but she doesn't let that stop her from enjoying life. Her talent is being able to manipulate paper. However, at the same time, she just wished she might be able to enjoy life to its fullest, to be able to do something meaningful. Just like everyone else.

Being the only bunny who does not have a calling, she would spend most of her time reciting from her spiritual book, and on occasion, she would go and help out at the papermaker's factory. Before she would leave, her mother would always come and wrap her arms around her in a hug. She would then whisper to her saying, "Sunshine, my lovely daughter, all is well; do not be discouraged, for it only means that the Lord has a greater purpose for you."

"I only hope so, Mother," said Sunshine, as she got her paper delivery ready. Such is the way of the bunny with no talents. The only person who was willing to take pity on her was the papermaker. He was the one who supplied paper for the entire warren, and Sunshine was his assistant. It was more out of pity than need that he allowed her to come and learn to make paper with him.

She secured her delivery to the wagon, the one she made herself, using her papermaking skills. It is amazing what a little piece of paper can do if the person has the knowledge of what to do with it. Sunshine was never a master of anything, but she was a quick learner of words and literacy.

Quickly taking her delivery, she left the den of the papermaker and went across the warren to the apprentice's den. This is where all of the apprentices spend most of their time learning their trade that is being taught to them.

After dropping off her delivery, she left the apprentice's den. Then not wanting to waste the day, Sunshine decided to go into the woods to gather more decarded tree bark. That way they would have plenty of material for paper making.

While on her way out of the warren, Sunshine came across a group of color apprentices practicing their trade, one of them being her sister. She looked upon them with longing in her eyes. "If I could master colors, then I could do something important for a change!" Taking her wagon, she hurried past them before she was noticed. Some of those students she had known from a child, but ever since their talents were discovered, it seems like they never have the time anymore. They were always too busy trying to create the perfect spring for Easter.

Sunshine stifled her sadness then continued on her way out of the warren. Unnoticed by her and everyone else, a slithering presence slunk through the brush. It came upon the practicing apprentices; then, as fast as lighting, it struck out and bit the foot of Sunshine's sister, Glowshine. Afterward, it shrank back into the dark from where it came.

Its job was now complete, and the apprentice who was bitten had no idea that she was the carrier of a great infection to their people.

A few days had passed, and Sunshine was hard at work making a new batch of paper when she noticed the lye was out. Once informing her master of the situation, she then grabbed her bag and went into the town market.

When walking down the first path, Sunshine noticed something was off. The road was unusually quiet that day. Normally, there would be bunnies passing by her all the time on their way to do their work. Sunshine walked into the town market to find the whole place deserted.

"This is very odd," said Sunshine, as she walked through the ghost town. It was so eerily quiet that it made the hairs on the back of her neck stand up. She quickly moved to the shop where the lye was sold. She thumped her foot at the shop entrance; this is a bunny's way of knocking, but no one answered.

Confused, Sunshine looked up at the sign only to find another smaller sign covering it instead. It read, "Sorry, I'm out sick right now. Please, come back later!"

Okay, no matter, thought Sunshine. *There are plenty of other shops that sell the same things.* She bounded off, checking all the other shops in the town market only to find that all the other shops had the same sign on them. That troubled Sunshine greatly, and immediately her thoughts went to her family. *Are they okay? What about my little sister?* Sunshine loved her mother and sister very much.

She bounded off so fast that her feet barely touched the ground. Running so fast until she came to the den of her family. She ran to the entrance and thumped her foot, but no answer came just like before. Sunshine braved the darkness of her own home and went inside.

She felt around for the lamp that was usually kept at the end of the table, but she couldn't find it. Instead, she reached into her bag and took out some paper and quickly wrote "glow" on it. Then, the paper became illuminated like a candle.

With the glowing paper in her hand, Sunshine made her way down the hall, lighting the lamps along the way. She then turned and went into the kitchen where she found her mother collapsed on the floor in front of the stove. Sunshine rushed over to her and tried to shake her awake, but she remained unresponsive. It looked as though she as in the middle of making some herb soup when she passed out.

Sunshine carefully picked her mother up, laid her in bed, and covered her up. Once she was sure that her mom was safe and comfortable, Sunshine went to the room across the way to see if her sister Glowshine was there. Opening the door, she looked inside and saw the room was empty. *Where is my sister?!* she thought, but then picked up her ears when she heard a hissing sound coming from the kitchen. "Oh, no!" said Sunshine, as she ran back to the kitchen to tend to the soup her mother had been making. She added the last bit of herbs that were missing from the recipe to finish the soup. Then, she put the lid on to let it boil down for a few minutes.

While waiting for the pot to boil, the room became quite hot. So, she opened the window to let some air in the house. Then, through that window came a certain kind of breeze; Sunshine picked up her ears, for she thought she heard a small voice dancing upon the wind. "What was that you said?" asked Sunshine. She could hear someone speaking, but she could not hear the words.

So, she listened closer and more intently. "Return …… that which was …… lost ….," said the small voice on the wind.

"Return? Return what?! I don't understand." Sunshine thought for a moment, but then was distracted by a whistling sound. She turned to see the pot boiling over. "Oh, no!" She ran over to take the pot off the fire. Checking the herb soup, she sighed saying, "Well, I hope Mom doesn't mind overcooked soup." She filled a bowl of soup and hurried and took it to her mother.

Walking into her mother's room, she saw that her mother had not moved from her bed where she had laid her. "Here, Mom. I finished the soup you were making. Please try to eat; it will help you feel better," said Sunshine, putting the bowl on the table dresser next to her mother's bed. Then sitting down, she took a spoon and began to gently feed her mother some of the soup. Once the bowl was emptied, she saw that her mother's strength had returned to her. Sunshine waited a moment to make sure she was okay. Then, she picked up the empty bowl and turned to walk away, but was stopped by her mother's voice.

"It must be returned," said her mother.

Sunshine turned around towards her mother and said, "What was that you said, Mom?"

"The phoenix feather, it must be returned."

"What do you mean?"

Her mother sat up and took a deep breath saying, "The night before I had the most peculiar dream of a feather floating across our land, and in its wake as it moved nothing but destruction followed in its path. Then at the end of the dream, I would here the phoenix lord's voice calling to me saying, 'Return my feather before the land is destroyed!'" Sunshine's mother shuffled uncomfortably, "I believe something has happened to the phoenix feather, my daughter. Do you remember the story of our history that is told?"

Sunshine shook her head slowly saying, "I don't remember much of it, why?"

"A long time ago. The bunnies of our ancestors were nothing more than the servants of the world. Destined with giving the world only nourishment throughout sacrifice. So, it was ordained from the beginning until a certain bunny from our ancestral line did something marvelous. There was a time when the great phoenix needed help and our ancestor, Jack was his name, decided to go and help out the great phoenix. It is said that the speed of a rabbit was needed in order to get a message to the everlasting mountain in time. It is not said what was done, for that part in our history is lost. However, the phoenix was so grateful for the help that was given that he in return gave a single feather to us. It is said that with the feather, we would be greatly blessed, and we were. We are no longer like the other rabbits of the world. We are more learned and creative. However, with all of these blessings come responsibility. The great phoenix also said, 'Anyone who doth use my gift for evil, no matter how small, thou shall be greatly cursed. If this were to ever happen then my feather must be returned to me with great haste! Lest the entire forest shall suffer!'"

"Why are you telling me this, Mom? Unless something happened to the feather?" asked Sunshine. "What should I do?"

"Follow the whispers in the wind. They shall not fail you."

"Mom, I can't leave you. You and our family are in no shape to be without assistance. I also can't find Glowshine; she seems to have disappeared."

"I do not know where Glowshine is. I thought she was in her room. She came home with a terrible fever. That was when I went to make some herb soup for her when I suddenly fell ill. Fear not though, we have already sent for help from the healer tribe. They are a part of the same line of bunnies who decided to break away and follow a different path, a path of healing both physically and spiritually. They now just travel around and help out whenever they can. Now, you must go before this sickness takes ahold of you as well."

Nodding her understanding, Sunshine ran to pack herself a bag of provisions. Among the provisions was a small stack of slips of paper and her brush that she used to write with. She then slung the bag over her shoulder and dashed out the front door.

She ran to the tallest grass mount in the land. Usually, that area was meant for ceremonies where the wind can dance freely all around everyone. She stood tall and pricked up her ears. *I am here! Speak to me,* she thought. As she did, there was a sudden wind that came dancing into the warren.

"Listen, listen, little one. Go to the south-most daylight. You will find what you seek." Once receiving this instruction, Sunshine dashed off in the direction of where the wind was taking her. She followed it faithfully, and it brought her to the southernmost gate of the warren. Sunshine hesitated at the entrance. She feared stepping through the threshold. The door had been blocked off since ancient times. Behind the door is an ancient wetland. It is a land that has been cursed due to selfishness and pride and has remained so even to this day. Not much has been known about what happened because that part of history is not taught. The only thing Sunshine knew was that what happened there was so bad that most don't wish to remember it.

"Do not fear! The house stays true to the whispers of the wind; then, the evil echo shall have no power over thee. Now, you must go save the one that is about to commit a fatal mistake!"

Receiving courage from that last statement, Sunshine crossed the threshold of the door. As she stepped through, her paws started to sink into the boggy earth. She looked out ahead to see the wetlands stretching out. Sunshine crouched down, gathering her feet underneath her; she then took a deep breath and marched off through the wetlands, running fast.

Sunshine was running so fast, and the only direction she had was from the whispers in the wind. All the scenery around her was a blur. "Thou must make greater haste; the evil echo is on thy heels."

When hearing that, Sunshine sprinted at full speed. Both her front and back legs were stretched out at full length off the ground. "Over there! Make haste down that hole!" Sunshine bolted down the nearest hole that was big enough for her to fit.

"You must hurry, little one. There down this hole is the one who needs guidance."

"Okay," said Sunshine, as she cautiously made her way down the old tunnel. Seeing the old carvings upon the wall, Sunshine knew they were from the color artists in its early days. For that was what they were tasked with, to make the warren beautiful. Finally coming out in the main part of the old warren, Sunshine saw a dimly lit light over the far corner. When investigating further, she saw in horror an unauthorized ceremony taking place.

Sunshine looked around. There was no one that she could see. She moved in closer to where the phoenix's feather lay on an altar. Just before she got to the altar, her foot made contact with something on the floor. Looking down, Sunshine saw a hooded figure laying upon the ground. She then hopped away as the figure began to move. The person in question stood up, turned to her, and sat down.

"Glowshine!" exclaimed Sunshine, when seeing who the hooded figure was. Sunshine then studied her for a minute; the bunny that sat down wasn't even looking at her but staring straight ahead at nothing.

Her eyes were blank, her face completely devoid of emotion. "Glowshine, my sister. Can you hear me!" The other bunny did not respond.

"No, my sister, no!" Sunshine cried. She then tried again by pulling out her notebook and placing it in her sister's lap. "Glowshine, please if you are still there. Please let me know!" she said, pushing her brush into her sister's hand and helping to form her fingers around it. Ever so slowly, Glowshine started to move the brush, writing down her words. Sunshine was filled with joy when she saw that. After a few minutes, her sister stopped moving the brush, and Sunshine took the notebook to see what she had drawn. The writing said: "Hello, my sister. I am sorry that I made you worry so much!"

"Glowshine, you know better! You have been taught to know that by abusing the one sacred gift will bring misfortune upon you."

"I am very sorry, my sister, but I was forced to do it."

"By who?!"

"By him! Look behind you!"

Sunshine turned around to find a huge snake staring down at her. "GASP! Who are you?"

"I am known as Graunda in my tribe, and I have been trying to get towards that feather over there! And I have this bunny right here to thank for performing this ceremony to try and dampen its flame for me."

"So, you were the one who poisoned everyone in the village."

"Yes, with my convincing poison that has the power to turn anybody's will. It was too easy for me to convince a least one of your kind to do my biding."

"I hope you know that a lot of people have suffered greatly because of you!"

"Save your preaching for someone who cares! For I have my own prophecy that I must fulfill. Now last chance, give me the feather or die by my bite right now!" said the snake.

"Allow him to have it for now, Sunshine, if his desire for it is really that great. Then, so shall be his responsibility for it as well," said the whispers on the wind.

"Okay, for some reason I feel it is okay to give you this feather right now, but before I do, I want to ask why you want it so badly."

"In my people's belief, a story has been told to us since we were hatchlings, and that is if one of us were to devour a feather of the phoenix, we shall gain the breath of fire. That is my dream to become a dragon upon the earth."

"If that is so your belief, then here," said Sunshine, holding out the feather to him.

"Finally!" said the snake, opening his mouth wide and swallowing the feather in one gulp. "Yes, I do feel the power within me!" Graunda hissed. Then, immediately he opened his mouth and blew out a breath of fire. Sunshine had no time to react; she was caught right in the midst of it.

Sunshine screamed in terror but soon realized that she wasn't getting hurt. The fire stood on her body all around, but it did not burn her.

"What is this?! Why do my flames not hurt you?"

"Because it is not your flame! That fire belongs to the phoenix, and his fire shall not hurt the innocent. But those who abuse the flame have everything to fear!" Sunshine said, reciting bit of text she had always remembered reading in the book of light even since childhood.

When she said that, almost as if in response to her words, the fire burst through the skin of the serpent. The snake screamed as the fire quickly engulfed him. Within seconds, there was nothing left but the phoenix's feather itself. Sunshine walked over and gave a light bow and asked, "Will you permit me to touch you?" Once she received the okay within her heart, she took out a small handkerchief and reverently wrapped it up and placed it in her pocket pouch of her backpack. "Come, let's get you back home where you will never be abused again."

Then, taking her sister by the shoulders, she gently raised her up and led her out of the old warren tunnel. Cautiously, she looked out to see if the coast was clear, for she remembered the unseen threat that chased her through the forest. The evil echoes were still out there. Sunshine perked up her ears; she could hear them laughing at her fear and talking in that horrible forbidden language. Just as this land had been cursed for its selfish desires, Sunshine feared that her homeland might be the same.

She was too afraid to step out. When suddenly, courage came into her heart by way of the whispering wind saying, "Do not fear little one. The light of the feather that you have is more than enough to keep these shadows at bay." With that, courage came to her heart once more. She stepped out onto the sodden earth, and she took two slips of paper where she wrote the word "haste" on them. Then, she wrapped them around her feet. She put her sister onto her back and dashed off back towards home with the help of the paper to give her a boost to her speed, so that way when she reached the warren again, she would not be so tired.

The two of them soon arrived safely back at Greenhill Village. "Finally, we are home," exclaimed Sunshine. Before going farther, she turned around where she tightly closed the door to the wetland, sealing it once more. Hopefully, it would never be disturbed never again. Afterward, she then took her sister and led her back into the village. When she got there, she saw the village was alive with healing bunnies all around, helping those that were afflicted by the illness. She walked up to one of these healers who just got through administering to one of the families. She uttered a greeting to him, "Thank you for all that you do, traveling healers. I have one who is in desperate need of your help," she said bringing Glowshine forward. One healer bunny took one look at Glowshine and immediately called for assistance. They all surrounded her, taking her away. Sunshine was worried as she watched them go but then turned and sped away. She had to see how her mother was doing.

However, the whispers of wind were still calling, reminding her that her adventure was not yet done. She ran speedily through the forest towards Everlasting Mountain, where it is said in stories the phoenix lord makes his home. "I must go quickly, and I will come back as soon as I am able."

She ran for the space of many days, finally collapsing underneath a bush. Her joints ached, and her lungs hurt from breathing so deeply. Sunshine looked up at the mountain. It was no closer than before when she started. *How is that possible? I have been running for a long time. I should be getting close by now; this forest is not that big!* she thought just before she fell into an unexhausted asleep.

In her dream, she was frolicking in a meadow when a voice came clearly to her. "Thou wishes entry into the mountain?"

"Yes, I do."

"Thou must know that the only way is to show thankfulness in reverence. Then, thy entry shall be assured," responded the voice.

The thought of that message Sunshine could not help but feel stupid for a moment. *Of course!* she thought. *How could I have forgotten?*

She then found a small clearing in the forest; there, she knelt down in reverence and gave an offering of prayer. With closed eyes, she prayed with all of her strength. When she opened them, she found herself standing in a green meadow. She looked up, and there on a tree branch, as if it were a throne, was the great phoenix!

His fiery majesty took her at awe in amazement. Sunshine walked up to him and gave a humble bow. Only after receiving his acknowledgment did she straighten up.

"I have watched, you, little one, and I say with complete confidence that no one has been as faithful in their journey as you have," the phoenix said with a smile.

Sunshine smiled at the compliment that was given to her and said "I am here to return your feather to you." Sunshine took out the feather and presented it to the phoenix.

"You should know that I shall not accept that feather. My gift has been misused."

"I am very sorry! I know from the stories that were told to me as a child that we are not worthy of this gift. So, I am here to return it as requested upon the wind."

The phoenix cocked his head to the side for a moment. "Never, since that time since I have been tasked with watching over the small ones, has one proved themselves worthy of this gift as you have." The phoenix hopped down from his branch. He then raised up his head and called a musical melody.

Immediately, there was a bright flash of white light, from the light came a being far grander than even the Phoenix. The phoenix was the first to speak, while the other being said nothing, but just looked expectantly at the phoenix.

"Oh, great star maker, you have asked me to bring you one who would be worthy of the gift of spring. Here is the one I believe who is worthy of such a gift."

The other being turned his stunning gaze onto her. Sunshine shrank down in fear. After studying her for a moment, finally he spoke. "Yes, I do believe you're right. I have watched what this little one has done and how she lives her life in perfect worthiness," said the white being, turning towards the phoenix.

There was a pleasant smile on his face, as he turned toward Sunshine and spoke to her. "Will you accept the gift of spring?" Sunshine immediately nodded her head.

"To the one little one, this great gift will come with great responsibility," said the phoenix.

"I trust your judgment if you believe me to worthy in your eyes," smiled Sunshine.

"Well said, little one," responded the white being. He then stepped forward as the phoenix stood near. He placed his hands upon her and said the words of blessing, "You are a great crafter of temporal things; now, we shall make you a great crafter of spiritual things in which thou shalt bring forth new life. We ask this gift to be upon you now and also upon all those who are deemed worthy to have such a gift as well."

Once the blessing was over, Sunshine brought up her head. She knew she was different, but she was unsure of how yet.

"Look upon the child," said the white being.

Sunshine looked; the white being began to do circles and twisting motions with his hands. Sunshine studied his movements for a moment; then with her own hands, she mimicked his motions. When doing so, suddenly there was an egg-shaped object in her hand. *What is this?* Sunshine thought at first, but then through her blessing, she suddenly knew what the object was. It was the spiritual egg made from godly matter. It is the essence from which life comes. Sunshine took her brush that she had with her and immediately drew a golden tree upon it.

The white being smiled. "I am very pleased to see that you have mastered your gifts so easily. We know that thou shall never use this gift in a selfish manner. When you get back to the village, take the fruit from the tree and feed it to your little sister. It shall heal her and help her grow strong just like you. Now go and do what thou have been blessed to do," said the white being before disappearing in a flash of white light.

The phoenix then came forward saying, "Now, I shall return you home where you will be known as Spring's blessing which shall be forever called Easter." The phoenix spread his wings. Sunshine climbed up onto his back, keeping her spirit egg safe with her, and in a flash of white light, they were in the air flying back to the village.

They landed in the middle of the warren meadow of Greenville Village. Sunshine hopped down from the phoenix's back, and as instructed, she buried the spirit egg into the ground. And in that very spot sprouted a magnificent golden tree with glowing white fruit hanging from its branches. For a moment, Sunshine was in awe but then reached up and picked one of the fruits from the branches. Putting it safely inside the pouch of her backpack, she turned and raced towards the infirmary. That is where the healing bunnies had taken those who were severely afflicted by the poison.

Remembering the words of the white being and knowing them to be true, Sunshine immediately ran to the room where her sister was. Opening the door, Sunshine looked inside to see her sister lying on her bed, and the healing bunnies were all around her doing what they could to try to take the affliction away from her. Sunshine moved over to the bed. She looked at her sister's face, which was still blank, and her eyes were still lost. She knelt down. She whispered, "I am here, and I have something for you that will help. It is from the golden tree outside. Please, take a bite."

In response to her words, Glowshine opened her mouth just slightly. Sunshine took out the fruit and put it up her sister's lips. After taking one bite, recognition came back into her eyes. "Sister?"

"Oh, Glowshine! I am happy that you are okay," Sunshine said hugging her sister.

"You said there is a golden tree outside? Can I see it?"

"Of course, come with me." They both took hands and went outside. Upon seeing the tree, there was a bright flash, and instantly Glowshine's body became like her sister's. Everyone who saw that happen rushed towards the tree and partook of the fruit. Suddenly, all the bunnies of the whole village were like unto what Sunshine was.

Then, with the planting of the golden tree and the transformation of the bunnies in the village, instantly there came a sudden transformation of the area in which all the bunnies lived because of everything that had happened. They were are no longer like the rest of the animals in the forest. As such, they no longer can be with rest of the forests of the world. The area, in which they now live, exists in a realm between hopes and dreams. The Spring bunnies, as they are now called, all took quickly to their new responsibilities of Easter. Sunshine went on with her life and passed on what was taught to her by the white being.

Every year when spring comes around, it is a most joyous time for these bunnies. For when the children of the world find the beautifully decorated eggs on Easter, they are happy for their little treasures that they find. However, for the bunnies, these are more than that; they are the new life that has begun again.

About the Author

Michelle Ball was born in the beautiful city of Redlands, California. She has worked diligently in receiving her degree in both Business and Computers. However, her true passion has always been writing. She has been writing short stories ever since she was in elementary school. She was often recognized by her teachers for her unique ability with words. She is now living a great life in Ogden, Utah with her brother and is always thankful for the chance to share her work with others.

M II

The Return Of The King

Written By D. C.

A POET IS, BEFORE ANYTHING ELSE, A PERSON WHO IS PASSIONATELY IN LOVE WITH LANGUAGE.

W.H. AUDEN

50 Powerful Quotes about Poetry   WordsDance.com

JUST RIGHT

Where did I, how did I come to find my Just Right, all through the days and nights, I think about my Just Right, the love we share, the way you take me there each and every time we become joined at the hip, giving me that lazy love, taking my mind on a trip you flip the script, you have me on tilt, drunk off your love, my Just Right; when I look upon you through your eyes, there's a feeling that comes over me on the inside, it's like a party has jumped off, staying hard never going soft when inside deep lost in your palace, I can't even imagine life without you; you have me doing things I normally won't do, falling victim to your love. You got that "I don't want to go nowhere" type of love, my Just Right sent from above, you're feeling so right my Just Right. I promise what I'm going to do tonight will ease your soul as I push through your spine; these feelings are so hard to fight going high taking flight, I'm reaching from deep down inside, my love is steadying at a climb, raising high, forever I want you to be mine, relaxing your mind as I unwind your body; at the end of this escapade, you will come to find why you can't find another Just Right, feelings are coming unraveled, breaking loose as I go through and through with my tongue pleasuring you, pleasing you my Just Right; tonight it's your night, from your Oh's and Ah's, I know you're feeling good inside, my body giving off that Just Right as I proceed to give you what you fiend, picking up my speed with my tongue feeding you your drug, as I dug I mean dig, calling out switch my Just Right grabs my royal stick to show me what she working with, showing me why she is my Just Right, giving it to me the way I like, kissing and licking down the side looking softly into your eyes as my toes begin to curl; it's about to get live, I want you girl, climb on top and drop me into your juice box, sliding in slow as you proceed to rock the boat now we on cruise control, yes a slow coast until you feel that undying flow, fast and faster you start to go, hitting your spot ready for that splash I grab your ass tightly as you release your passion, tonight will be an everlasting memory; you just watch and see I have a few tricks up my sleeve, yelling out switch so I can continue to make you weak in the knees as I proceed I drop back to my knees pulling you towards the edge of the bed; no, no, no I don't need any guidance; get your hands off my head (smiles) I got this watch this as I suck and lick, lick and suck, kiss with a soft touch of my tongue with a twist I flip you over to pick you up now I'm licking you deep while I stand up my Just Right I told you this will be passion and love all night, you feel my strength and my might as you play with my royal mic, putting you down so I can give you what you like, what you will love once I am done, I'm the one, the only, the King of your palace no one can match this as I flip and twist your body in positions you never been in before my love you I want to explore, adore this passion we dishing no more hoping and wishing my Just Right, I want to show you this type of love for life, show you how it really feels to be loved by someone who's real, my heart I spill for you my special girl you are my world as I give your body a twirl pulling out to play with your pearl, in you I found a winner; are you ready to run your victory lap flipping you over so I can go deep, from the back slow with my attack you throwing it back, arch deep down the middle, picking up the pace just a little, you're giving me what I need, feeding of your vibe, no way my feelings can hide, this love making will go all night until the morning sun, weak I have become in my knees staying deep in between, you're ready to cum you scream, so am I my Just Right as we drift off into an Unforgettable Night.

YOUR CURVES

The greatest thing created here on this earth is a woman and her curves. If you haven't explored it, then you got some nerves. Let me explain how it works; all your gears will come into play; be careful some will have you steering the wrong way, kissing on her face to those lips, ready I am for this road trip, closing the door starting my engine, so I can dip through Your Curves, doing the speed limit for now going down your neck coming to a steep hill to climb, putting my car in overdrive, teasing your feelings inside as I go around and around your breasts; my car runs off nothing, but the best, coming up on your road sign saying don't speed around these curves, you will crash, it gets slippery when wet, so I can't smash the pedal to the floor just yet, no passing in this single lane, hitting every spot with a lot of tongue lashing down your highway of love, coming out of those hills and curves a straight shot, as I merge left into the fast lane with the way my tongue moves in between, you will have no complaints passing up your waist, touching you in that right place, giving you what you need as I proceed to speed through your highway, overjoy is read across your face, one point five miles before I take my place, filling your space, a half mile until you cum, giving you that A1 until the sun comes up, exiting onto a different part of Your Curves, no blurred lines here, I see your love real clear, entering your stratosphere taking away your fear, hands firm on your steering wheel, deep you feel my thrust going fast like I'm in a rush, nope my tires won't bust until we reach your destination, turning up the A/C, it's getting hot in here like that Greenlight Special or that Until You Climax, Body To Body, pedal down to the max, cracking that two hundred on the dashboard, forever adore Your Curves, breaking your back with how I attack, giving you what you deserve, going hard and fast, you flying high and above uplifting your spirits, shifting gears, your destination is close, we're

near, clenching your thighs pushing inside for the rest of the night
Your Curves will be all mine.

ROYAL CHALLENGE

*Back at it again, yes you know you will win when dealing with King,
but I got something new I want to put on your mind, we're going to do
this thing a little different tonight, let me take this time to explain my
Royal Challenge, my mind works in ways you can't imagine, never
seen before, yes I am yours, but I need you to challenge me sexually,
mentality, stimulate my soul, so that I would never want to let go, give
me that forever hold, Ready, Set, Go, I need you to be me, and I will be
you tonight, we're Trading Places, for years I've been telling you,
showing you how I'm going to treat your body, make love to your mind
and soul, giving you rounds for every second spent away from you,
taking your heart to never break, to never let go, I'm that number one
under the sun, you do whatever it takes for my Royal Challenge to be
all up in your body, to become one, giving me that undeniable show,
can't no one replace the things I can do, giving you that Reminder with
the moves I possess, yes this is a test, I hope you pass, listen closely,
my love is your devotion, so I challenge you not to feel any emotion
after all my stroking and teasing, playing with your vibe, you know
what I hold inside this lightning and thunder when I give you that
royal steel, you feel what I feel that is real my love tingling through
your vibes, I challenge you not to look me in the eyes as I spread your
legs wide to dip slip inside of your palace, that love deep in your
Passion, freaky emotions are flowing in the air, you can't help but
stare into my eyes, there lies the feelings through your eyes, so sexy
and sensual, seducing, grabbing my full attention while at full
attention still stroking with a slow stroke, I go and go, giving you that
Royal Show, this my challenge, you have to take these 9 and a half
long and thick from the back, watch the script flip, you can't moan or
scream, looking at me with that mean sexy face, your body I'm about
to do great, wait arch that back your left ass cheek I smack, quick with*

my attack then I slow it down, passion frowns, love faces, your waterfall is racing you can't hold on to the challenge as I push deep with a hard thrust you let out a loud scream and moan as you bust like never before, I'm giving you a drug that you will feign for, hitting your core, exploring your world, making you erupt, after tonight you will want to be my girl, have me for all time to yourself, my Royal Challenge has been dealt, You Never Felt A Feeling Like This Before, next time be sure you're ready to endure this Everlasting ride, keep me on your mind until next time.....

ON REPEAT

The first time I held you close, we raised our glasses to make a toast, I don't want to brag or boast, but I did the most to your body, I had you feeling some type of way, at first you weren't trying to fall, you didn't want to stay, you curved it all, until I unlocked that hidden treasure, digging into your soul, going places no one else can go, you tapping my butt whispering go baby go, make me explode, putting my groove into overdrive, your water fall has arrived, On Repeat baby as I Turn you to your side, lifting your thigh so that I can slide through your puddle of love, oh what have I done, sprung you are going to become, I am the one who can have you On Repeat in one session, I'm giving you a Lesson In Love, putting it down in so many ways. I have your body doing the wave, as I stroke your everglades, this love, my love will sway your feelings my way, yes you are going to want to stay in this place I call my Kingdom below my waist, this taste I'm giving is like none other, drowning in your puddle under these covers, I am that lover they call King, making you fiend for my drug as you scream out number two, I'm giving my best to you, none can do you like me, I told you I can have you On Repeat in one session, confessing your love you are, smiling brighter than the stars, far from done, hard and stiff, come climb my mountain, place, slide my fully equipped into your palace, cruising slow, hitting every wall, making them fall as you quicken your pace, faster with your flow, yes baby go, popping that ass and dropping it low, showing me that freaky side, reverse cowgirl, damn is that right, you're letting your inner animal free, out the cage you are, looking back at it, you getting it I say while smacking your ass to your motion, at the very moment you explode, I told you I can have you On Repeat in one session, this here was your lesson, Putting All Your Expectations To Rest, tomorrow you can call your girls and tell them I'm the best you ever had, my Royal Love will never leave you mad, dissatisfied looking through your eyes past your heart to your soul, anytime you want me to hold you close, all you have to do is give me a signal like batman, I am that man who can have you On Repeat on any given night my love is just that right, oh what a night.

PALACE OF PLEASURE

Your Palace of Pleasure becomes a stormy weather when I start to move up your thighs, staring into your eyes moving closer so you can feel Mr. Right doing your body nice and slow, once I start to go performing my best show kissing you slow, putting your passion on cruise control, in control I am, ripping off your clothes so I can invoke your pleasure from the top of your head to the bottom of your feet, precious you are to me, as my tongue begins to dig deep inside your inner thighs, about to take you on a never-ending ride, for when I'm done and you're alone closing your eyes you will feel, see, smell me inside, leaving an impression on your life, with the way my love goes, my tongue just flows in and out, around and around, seducing your palace, licking and tongue kissing your lips that are between your hips, your wetness is dripping from my chin, I'm going deep within your pleasure, showing you I can weather your storm, pinning your legs back towards your head, in the middle of my bed, your hands rubbing on my head with moans and groans, legs begin to shake, that undying flow is about to come on, licking it all up, sucking on your lips while you erupt, I'm coming up to all smiles, it's about to get wild, you spread your legs with your finger you gesture to come closer, as I slide in all your moisture, Palace Of Pleasure, we French kiss, as I hit that spot, stopping I will not, pinning your arms to the bed, wrapping your legs, deeper I head in with short extended burst, my beautiful lady, I'm giving you all my worth, as we change positions, I place your legs on my shoulders, letting your arms go as I raise to extend in that pushup position, no more hoping and wishing, what you're about to feel is real, touching spots that you thought were lost, going soft until you can take it all, you will go through withdraws when I'm not in between your walls, lost in your sauce I become, harder I go breaking your bricks, no tapping baby, I won't quit, giving you that yellow light stick shift, going slow again, half in with just the tip, here comes that Greenlight Special again, as I rip through your Palace Of Pleasure, I can handle whatever you pitch, as we switch, flipping you over to hit you with my extended clip, with my hands gripping your ass firmly, spreading you widely, sliding right in again with that yellow light special, soon you will feel the might and power I hold, you grab a pillow to hold, as I go slow, a little deeper, but slow, it's almost that time for me to hit the gas and go, but for now I'm going to Take My Time and go slow so you feel how deep my strokes will go, coasting, flowing, I'm knowing you're loving these pleasure acts, the way I'm about to attack will put me where your heart is at, here we go, I know you didn't think I would come this hard, picking up my flow, petal to the floor, arch in your back so I can go deeper into your core, giving you more of what you deserve, some real back and forth action, splashing in your pool of love, pulling your head up by your hair so we can stare into the mirror, I want to see those love faces you make as I Break You Down, in me you have found a real King who wears the crown of real love making, back breaking, headboard shaking, my strokes are escalating, before I start to shaking I turn you around quickly wrapping your legs to my waist, taking my place in your palace, showing strength, picking you up, Lift Off into your Palace Of Pleasure, I can't measure, going where no one has ever taken you before, turning you out, as you scream and shout, as I bust into your Palace Of Pleasure house, giving you more than enough to talk about with your girls, you can't get enough of how I just rocked your world.

*****YOU HAVE JUST READ 5 SELECT POEMS FROM

THE RETURN OF THE KING

A COLLECTION OF POEMS BY D. C.*****

*****TO READ THE COMPLETE COLLECTION, YOU CAN PURCHASE A

COPY AT BARNESANDNOBLE.COM OR AMAZON.COM*****

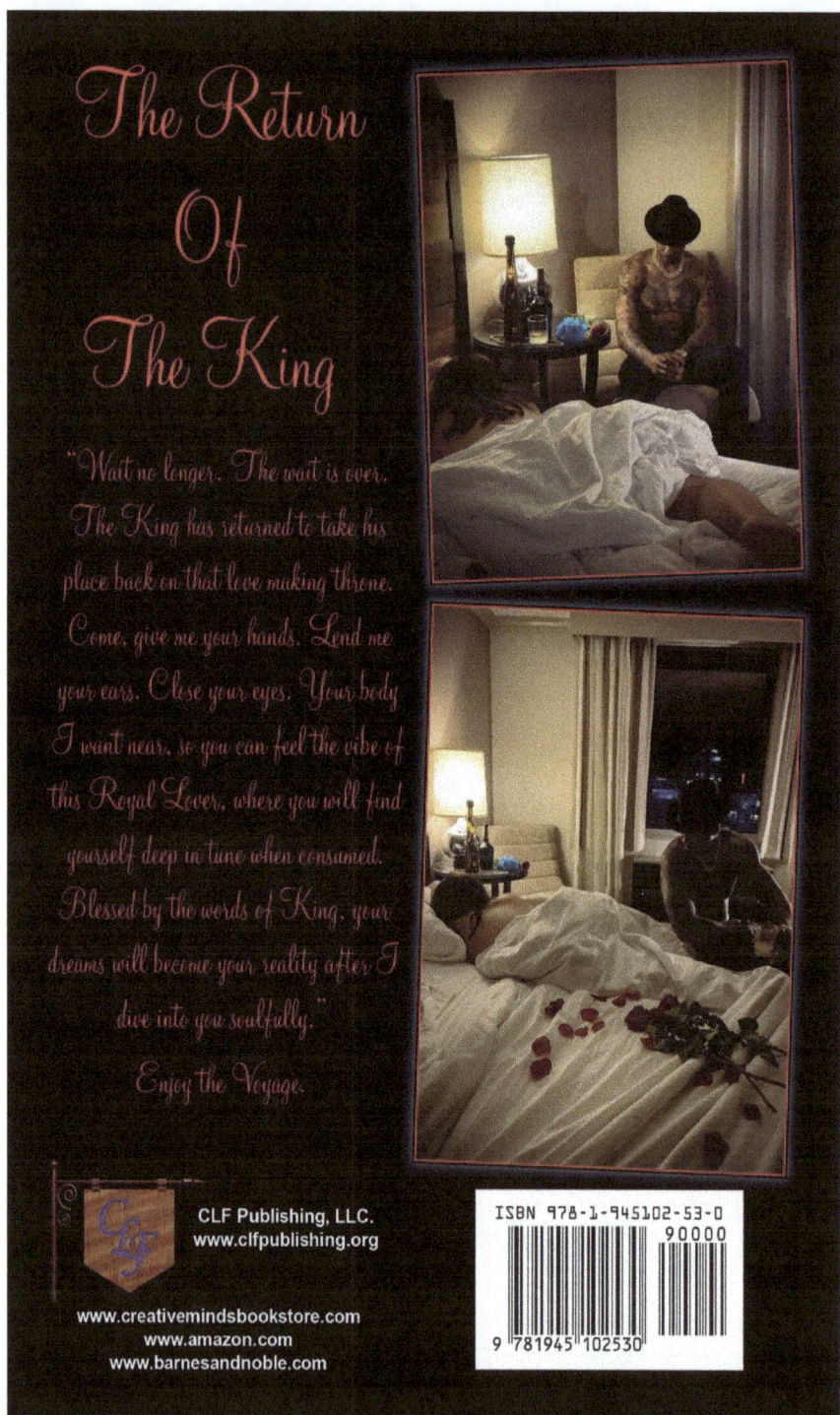

The Return Of The King

"Wait no longer. The wait is over. The King has returned to take his place back on that love making throne. Come, give me your hands. Lend me your ears. Close your eyes. Your body I want near, so you can feel the vibe of this Royal Lover, where you will find yourself deep in tune when consumed. Blessed by the words of King, your dreams will become your reality after I dive into you soulfully."

Enjoy the Voyage.

CLF Publishing, LLC.
www.clfpublishing.org

www.creativemindsbookstore.com
www.amazon.com
www.barnesandnoble.com

ISBN 978-1-945102-53-0
90000
9 781945 102530

Where is My Wife?

Crystal Marie Czarniak

Ode to Friendships

Friends...

They're the few people who accept silence over conversation.

A relationship like this denies silly promises and persuasion.

You don't feel the need to second guess thoughts or measure words.

Their love comes in wholes, not halves, not thirds.

They're the ones that guide you through when fate takes a turn.

Fights, small and large, end in forgiveness, never a burn.

You forget about first impressions and the feelings they brought.

You're grateful for who they are and you forgive 'em for

what they're not.

Kayla Rae Rich

As the doctor delivered the diagnosis, "He is in the beginning stages of Alzheimer's," Betty felt fear and relief at the same time. She was fearful for her husband's future and relieved the disease now had a name.

Gerald had been a well-known and very respected orthodontist, in a very large religious community. He was an only child that had been raised in a strict religious home. He was handsome in an unconventional way; he had a small jaw, large eyes, and a thick head of hair. When Gerald met his future wife, he knew she was perfect for him in every way.

Betty was tall with blonde hair and striking blue eyes. She was one of five girls raised in a small community. Even though she was in college, she didn't have plans on having a professional career. She wanted to get married and make a home for her husband and children just like her mother. Betty had had many boyfriends; she went to dances with her sisters and to church socials. She enjoyed necking with the boys but never went too far. She was a respectful young woman with a high value on her virginity. She had no idea that her choice for a husband would change her life and values.

Curtis had been a building contractor; he had one younger brother that he hadn't seen in years. He was raised by a single mother who was less than present. He never knew his father and claimed he never cared. He was a very large man, standing at 6'6" and 250 pounds, muscular with black hair and brown eyes. When Curtis hired Margaret to be his secretary, he had no idea she was going to be the love of his life.

Margaret was average size, but that was the only average thing about her. She was the youngest and the only girl of three children. She was intelligent and not afraid to express her opinion. Curtis found her to be simply irresistible. The more they worked together, the less control he felt over his feelings. He wanted her more every day, and he was determined to make her his. Margaret was indifferent about Curtis and was quite surprised by his advances. She would have hoped to have a career and enjoy her independence. She didn't know that marrying Curtis would end her independence and begin his dependence on her.

It was a beautiful day at the Cornville Home for Alzheimer patients. The facility was elegantly decorated and furnished with a beautiful color scheme of navy blue and gold. All of the employees were dedicated to the care of the residents and had been there long term. It was the best facility within the State of California and was highly rated. The kitchen employed a four-star chef, so every meal was a delight. The sky was blue outside in the courtyard, the birds were singing, and the day room was filled with all the residents.

Every Wednesday, Karen, the occupational therapist, would come and work with the residents. She tossed the ball around the room with little participation. She would call out each of their names as she tossed the ball to them. She would recite the ABC's in a song and count to 20, trying to get interaction from the residents. Karen was thirty years old and had personal experience with her grandmother's diagnosis five years prior. Karen's grandmother also lived in Cornville. She was in this room with her granddaughter when her grandmother asked her what her name was. Karen held her emotions back and answered. In this room, Curtis and Gerald sat in the circle unresponsive when the ball was tossed in their direction.

Gerald had arrived at Cornville six months prior, after two years of home care. The onset of Alzheimer's had been slow at first with him just forgetting patients' names. He started putting his socks in the dishwasher to dry. Betty had been concerned about Gerald's ability to drive. He had ended up at the local gas station and didn't remember where he lived. The diagnosis was bitter sweet and had been the answer to Betty's prayers. Betty had her suspicions but was cautious to approach Gerald with them. Throughout their marriage, Gerald controlled every aspect of their life together.

Betty was treated as if she was a child herself at times; he would punish her by taking away what he considered her privileges. Gerald would tell her that she had disappointed him with her behavior and he would take away her checkbook and credit cards. What Gerald didn't know was that Betty had totally separated her finances from the beginning. Betty had been very disappointed and unhappy with marriage from the start. She had hoped for a partnership that would support her dreams for her family and an eventually a career. She was pregnant with her first child within a month after their marriage, so she felt an obligation to stay. After giving birth to her son, she spent most of her time taking care of him. She found joy in being a new mother.

Gerald became jealous of her time and made sure his rules were followed. He would put their son to bed at 7pm every night and made sure Betty knew not to make it a minute later. Gerald would critique every aspect of their lives together. Gerald always felt he knew best no matter what. Betty had their second child, a daughter, two years later. She was happy with her two children and had no desire to have anymore. Gerald, on the other hand, planned to have a child every two years. Betty did not feel as she had a choice even if it was her body. Gerald would call her into the bedroom every night to have sex with him. Betty felt a knot in her stomach when he would call out to her. Betty wanted to travel, but Gerald would not leave his practice for more than a day at a time. Gerald worked six days a week and had a high turnover of staff.

Curtis had been a resident at Cornville for two years. His symptoms started with a slow loss of eyesight in his left eye. Curtis was a strong businessman that had a thriving construction business with over a hundred employees all across the state of California. His employees appreciated his honest and fair management style. Curtis started to have an issue with making decisions at home, and then, it progressed into his inability to make business decisions. Next, Curtis started having speech issues. He would start a sentence and forget what he was going to say before he started to speak. He suffered multiple breakdowns. He would yell and cry at the same time and finally had to sell his business.

When Curtis and Margaret had gotten married, they both hoped for a family within the first year of marriage. Five years later, they both had given up and no longer spoke of having children. Curtis started drinking after two years and isolating himself from Margaret. Margaret felt more like a caregiver than a wife. Curtis would not touch Margaret in any way, and they grew apart. They lived in a beautiful home that was filled with sorrow and disappointment. Margaret had starting teaching yoga and traveled to India searching for spiritual guidance. Margaret knew Curtis was depressed, and she tried to talk to Curtis about getting help prior to his diagnosis of Alzheimer's.

After receiving the diagnosis, Margaret had to face that she could no longer take care of Curtis. So, she researched to find not only the best but the closest care facility. Margaret had mixed emotions about putting Curtis in such a place. But she had a huge sense of relief after many months of Curtis ending everyday crying hysterically at home. He was a large man, so at times she would just lie on the floor with him waiting for him to stop crying and to fall asleep. After many months of that, Margaret knew he needed more capable care.

Every day after occupational therapy, the Cornville residents got corralled into the dining room. Karen, the therapist, would push her grandmother's wheelchair to her spot and then assist all the other residents into their seats. The dining room had large windows leading out to a courtyard filled with beautiful blooming trees. It was spring, and the weather in California was beautiful. Betty and Margaret had seen each other in the dining room on multiple occasions before they had introduced themselves. Margaret was always a little leery of other women that started conversations with a children and grandchildren count, because she had none. Even though she had considered adoption, she felt it would not be in a child's best interest to be in a home filled with sorrow. Margaret had a bohemian sense of style that was colorful but sensible. She would dress with her yoga leotard under a long flowing skirt with large patterns. Margaret had long hair pulled into a ponytail.

Betty was shy when meeting other women that had careers. She had spent her life as a housewife and felt inferior to career woman. Betty had always wanted to have the freedom to have a career in finance. She had managed to invest her inheritance and now was a millionaire of her own accord. She was always conservatively dressed with high collars and flat shoes in neutral colors. But Betty did wear red lipstick that made her feel feminine; it was a beautiful contrast. Betty also wore tortoiseshell glasses that she wore low on her noise.

On the day the ladies introduced themselves, they had been forced to sit together. Curtis sat in Gerald's seat in the dining room. He looked at Margaret while sitting next to Betty and asked her, "Do you know where my wife is?" Both women looked at each other and started to giggle. They both realized that neither of their husbands no longer knew who either of them where. After that happened, the women had become friends, sharing their Alzheimer's progression stories. They made plans weekly to get together after they both visited their husbands.

At lunch, Margaret and Betty shared many of stories of their lives filled with ups and downs and how they had both been disappointed with the reality of marriage. Betty admitted she had felt like a prisoner and that she had always wanted to travel. Margaret admitted she had felt like a failure not having children. Both Betty and Margaret enjoyed the freedom to be honest and genuine with each other.

Karen, the therapist, noticed that the two women had become friends. Karen worked at a nearby senior center that had guided tours for seniors. Karen gave both ladies a copy of a flyer for a trip to Palm Springs. It was a weekend getaway with a guided tour of old Hollywood stars homes and a trip on the Sky Tram. Karen told both ladies, "You should go together. Why not? It could be fun." Betty had never been to Palm Springs, even though it was only two hours away. Margaret, on the other hand, had been to Palm Springs many times for yoga events.

After visiting with their husbands, Betty and Margaret met up for lunch. Betty felt reluctant to go away for a weekend. "What if Gerald needs me?" she asked. Margaret started laughing. "Oh, did you forget he doesn't know who you are?" Margaret reminded Betty, "He has been asking you for three months if you know where his wife is. Come on, we can do this. I know several great places to eat, and we can go shopping and buy you some flip flops."

Betty felt a sense of recklessness. "Oh, why not? We can do this. But I don't know about those flip flops. Aren't those for hippies?"

Margaret made the reservations and offered to pay. Betty wouldn't hear of it. "This trip is on me. Every penny of it!" Margaret was amused by the jester and called Betty a control freak.

The ladies' weekend was an event of mutual sharing. Both had missed out on so much in their marriages. At the end of the weekend, they both realized that even though they had different lives, they shared many similar experiences. While sharing, they would laugh and tease each other. Betty confided in Margaret her nightly routine of having to have sex with Gerald, and Margaret responded, "Now your bragging." Both women had a mutual respect for one another.

Betty shared how much she had enjoyed being a mother of little children and how much she disliked having her children judge her now as adults. When she had put Gerald into Cornville, she knew she could no longer care for him. Her daughter accused her of giving up on her father, and her son told her he couldn't help pay for it. Neither of them has tried to come visit their father. Betty was glad she only had two children and that she had secretly taken birth control to prevent any more pregnancies.

Margaret had shared that by year five of her of marriage she started an affair. She had wanted to leave Curtis, but she felt so much guilt, she just couldn't bring herself to leave. The affair had continued until Curtis became ill, and she felt obligated to take care of him. Margaret realized that she did love Curtis enough to make him as comfortable as possible in the few years he had left.

Upon returning from Palm Springs, the ladies met up again the following week. Cornville had turned into a second home for them. They both looked forward to seeing each other and sharing the events of the past week.

Betty had been busy selling her home and buying a small condominium. Margaret had retired from teaching yoga and also sold her house and moved into the same condominium complex as Betty. The two ladies started going to Cornville together once a week and having lunch out after. One year later, Gerald passed away, and Margaret met Betty's children at the funeral. Betty's children never did visit their father at Cornville. After Gerald's death, Betty started to realize she liked different foods. Betty had always prepared meals that her family liked. She gave up red meat and started a yoga class for strengthening. Betty knew she needed to learn how to take care of herself.

After Gerald's death, Betty continued to go to Cornville with Margaret weekly. Betty's investments continued to grow, and she continued to invest. Betty started buying small apartments first in Breezy Point, New York, then Coral Springs, Florida and finally Argeles-sur-Mer, France. Margaret enjoyed hearing about interest rates and the Dow Jones' ups and downs. Betty and Margaret had grown into a sister-like friendship. They both had dreams of traveling together in the future.

Curtis passed away two years later, after a long struggle with pneumonia. Margaret felt a sense of relief for him and his steady deterioration. Margaret had a small gathering after Curtis's funeral. All of his former employees attended. Margaret felt no regret for making the decision to care for Curtis. She knew that he was a good man at heart. Margaret and Betty, both still in their sixties, decided to travel from one location to the other. Their first trip was to France. Both ladies had always wanted to travel to Europe. As they packed their bags, Betty gave Margaret a tube of red lipstick. You know the French like red lips. Margaret tried the red lipstick on before packing it.

Margaret was a little apprehensive about wearing such a bold shade. Betty reassured her that she looked fabulous.

They traveled together for the next fifteen years, enjoying the freedom. One trip they would drive across the United States in a rental car and then fly down south to Florida and drive back to California. Every time they left, they changed how and where. They would take a flight to France and stay four months and take a cruise in Europe before returning to the United States. Every trip was different from the last. Both ladies planned each new adventure together. This continued on until the end of their lives.

About the Author

Crystal Marie Czarniak a former governmental representative that served families. Her writing career has been varied including legal, educational and technical writing. She has written several nonfiction articles on many topics for publication. She has a diverse background including being a medical caregiver to becoming a grief counselor after the passing of her dear son. She is a lifelong resident of Southern California. She enjoys living near the ocean because this is where she can clear her mind and find Peace in her heart. Crystal has a novel and self-help book in the works.

"Mastering others is strength,
Mastering yourself is true power."

Lao Tzu

Claire's Daughter

All families experience some type of drama at one time or another. However, some families experience drama more often than others. Later though, that same drama can be laughed at over Thanksgiving and Christmas dinners years down the road. In other cases, thoughts of the drama will always bring tears, feelings of pain and/or regret, or sadness. Claire's experience falls in the category of the latter.

From 1971-74, when Claire was only fourteen through seventeen years old, a time of her life when she was experiencing the joys and pains of transitioning from puberty into womanhood, she experienced a life-altering situation that would change her life forever. Unbeknownst to her entire family, her mother's husband, the man she knew as Suga Daddy, began raping her when Claire's mother was away from the home. After the first occurrence, Claire told her mother in hopes her mother would do something to prevent the travesty from occurring again. However, to Claire's surprise and disappointment, her mother did not believe Claire's accusation. Claire, having nowhere to go and no one she could turn to, continued to reside in the home. Her lack of shelter elsewhere was the perfect situation for Suga Daddy, as that gave him continued access to her.

So, unfortunately, the rapes continued. On one specific occasion, while Claire was in the act of being sexually assaulted, her older sister walked into the room and witnessed their stepfather on top of Claire. Horrified, she grabbed an icepick and commenced to stabbing Suga Daddy, commanding that he immediately cease the cruel act he was committing upon her sister. Feeling the sharp, excruciating pains that infiltrated his body, Suga Daddy moved away from Claire in horror, seeking shelter from his attacker.

The wounds Suga Daddy received at the hands of his victim's sister sent him to the emergency room. When Claire's mother learned of what her husband had done and why he was in the hospital, she still did nothing to protect her daughter from being sexually abused. But, at that point, she did not need to intervene and protect Claire because although Suga Daddy remained in the home, with Claire and the rest of the family, he refrained from touching her.

Years later, when Claire was in her late twenties or early thirties, she began to date a young man named Matthew. Together, Matthew and Claire desired to build a life together. At the time, Claire was still living at home with her mother and stepfather. Eventually though, Claire and Matthew moved from their respective residences and rented an apartment together. Matthew took care of the majority of the financial responsibilities by working a job and selling drugs on the side. Claire, on the other hand, braided hair (which she had done for many years) to provide her own income. A few months later, Claire became pregnant and eventually gave birth to a daughter. Life progressed while Matthew worked and continued his hustle and Claire took care of the baby.

A typical day in Claire's life consisted of braiding hair- one client after the other- and taking care of her beautiful daughter. But, one fateful day in March of 1980 would prove to be drastically different. It would be a day no one would forget for the rest of their life.

Matthew was out making his drug rounds, driving through the streets of Pomona with a broken taillight. That was all that was needed to capture the attention of a local police officer. Behind Matthew's car, the lights on the police car flashed, and the siren sounded. In a panic, he pulled over but was fearful of being arrested for drug possession with the intent to sell. With haste, he swallowed the drugs (PCP), attempting to conceal them from the officers.

Matthew's plan did not go as anticipated. Yes, he avoided being arrested for drug possession, but what transpired after-ward was not something Matthew could have ever predicted. Swallowing the drugs caused his blood stream to be flooded with deadly toxins. Slowly, Matthew became intoxicated by the drug. Not long after, he reached the home he shared with Claire and their daughter, relieved that the traffic stop did not turn out worse and that he had not been arrested.

When he entered the home, he greeted Claire in his normal manner and went along with business as usual. Slowly, his temperament changed, and Claire noticed how he began to act and speak in a strange manner. She had never witnessed such behavior from Matthew before. Out of nowhere, he began to mistake Claire for a demon or a monster. In his state of paranoia, he began attacking her. Claire had no choice but to defend herself against the threat of a wild man. To ward off his attacks, she picked up an ashtray and hit him with it. Instead of continuing to attack Claire, Matthew turned his attention to their three-month old daughter who was sitting in her car seat, which was positioned on the couch.

Looking down at his daughter, who he thought was another monster or demon, he pulled her from her car seat and began swinging her around, shaking her, and choking her. Claire screamed and screamed and screamed. Nothing she did or said could stop Matthew's erratic behavior. Before Claire could stop Matthew, he opened the front door of their apartment and had begun to descend the stairs with their daughter in his hands. As he ran down the stairs, he continued assaulting the baby by hitting her small, fragile body against the stairs' railings, causing further harm to her head, torso, and overall body. Unfortunately, that was not the extent of her injuries. Her father also dropped her to the ground, causing her to hit her head. He was treating her as though she was nothing more than a rag doll.

In the midst of the commotion, a good Samaritan was riding by on a motorcycle. Hearing strange noises, the motor-cyclist looked over at Matthew to see what the strange sounds were that he was hearing. The motorcyclist witnessed the devastation that was occurring right before his eyes. To bring an end to the dreadful and deadly series of events, the motorcyclist ran his bike directly into Matthew, attempting to cause an immediate cease to his actions and to save the baby who was obviously in harm's way. After being hit with the bike twice, Matthew dropped his daughter and ran away, seemingly to protect himself from harm. Others eventually heard the commotion and ran outside, but any efforts of assistance they may have attempted to render were futile. The baby girl was severely injured, and her injuries immediately caused her earthly demise.

Sometime later, the coroner, the police, and the paramedics showed up, but Matthew was not present at the scene. Consequently, the police were required to detect his location. When he was discovered, he was completely nude and attempting to hide out in a section of rose bushes on the campus of a nearby junior high school. Noticing Matthew's erratic behavior, the police officers took him into custody but decided he required medical attention. So, paramedics placed Matthew inside an ambulance and whisked him away to the hospital. With the criminal element embedded in Matthew's situation, police cars followed the ambulance to the hospital, as he legally remained in their custody. At the hospital, it was learned that Matthew had consumed PCP, and the drugs had made him hallucinate, which led to the incident with his family.

Days later, after the drugs were cleared from Matthew's system, he was remanded into the custody of the State of California. Charges were brought against Matthew, and a trial was scheduled. At the end of the trial, Matthew was convicted of second-degree murder (non-premeditated murder/man-slaughter) and sentenced to seven years within a state prison of which he served the full term.

Not long after Matthew was sent to prison, Claire began counseling to help her deal with the grief of losing both her three-month old daughter to death and her long-time boyfriend to prison. The entire string of events had occurred suddenly and were unfathomable. The events caused Claire to go into a tailspin, feeling very lost and confused and without comfort. Unfortunately, counseling alone was not enough to ease Claire's woes, so her psychiatrist prescribed psychotropic medication to assist in Claire's recovery of her mental and emotional state. As time drew on, Claire continued to experience severe depression and eventually turned to street drugs to self-medicate, hoping she could lose herself and her pain in the euphoria created by drug inducement.

Then, on a quiet and seemingly normal day, Claire encountered Jacob, an old friend with whom she had gone to high school. Their chance meeting led to a one-night stand. The one-night stand was the extent of their "relationship." Jacob was already in a long-term relationship with a woman named Shonna, and they already had a child together, so he was not looking for anything permanent with Claire. During that same time frame, Claire was continuing counseling and had even forgiven Matthew for his actions that had led to their daughter's death. Their relationship flourished, and they were married while

Matthew was still incarcerated. Because of the marriage, Claire and Matthew were permitted conjugal visits.

Not much later, Claire learned that either the visits with her new husband or her fling with Jacob had led to her second pregnancy. Claire was unsure which man had fathered her unborn child, but she told her husband the unborn baby was his, hoping her words were true. Time, however, would not fail to reveal the truth. When the time came to deliver, Claire gave birth to a healthy beautiful baby daughter.

I am that daughter. I am Phoebe.

Claire is my mother.

The baby girl who died much too early was the big sister I never had the pleasure to meet. It was her death that eventually led to my life coming to be.

If Matthew had not gone to prison, Claire would have probably never had a fling with Jacob, and I would have never been born.

You see, Jacob is my father, not Matthew.

And, this is my story.

*****YOU HAVE JUST READ CHAPTER 1 OF
MORE THAN JUST A BRAIDER,
A NOVEL BY THESE HANDS*****

*****TO READ THE COMPLETE NOVEL, YOU CAN PURCHASE A COPY AT
BARNESANDNOBLE.COM OR AMAZON.COM*****

When tragedy struck Claire's life, it sent her into a tailspin, one that would consume her for the rest of her days. Then, that same tragedy catapulted the birth of a new life, the life of her daughter Phoebe. As Phoebe's life takes form, no one can anticipate what path she will take.

Will the foundation she was born on be the reason she crumbles or the reason she succeeds?

Will it serve to determine the outcomes of the obstacles she will face?

Will it be her strength, her weakness, her downfall, or her uprising?

Phoebe's story is the true account of the first two decades of a young woman's life.

It will inspire you, touch your heart, and give you pause, all at the same time.

Stay tuned for Volume III!

CLF Publishing, LLC.
www.clfpublishing.org

These Hands' books are available at:
www.creativemindsbookstore.com
www.amazon.com
www.barnesandnoble.com

ISBN 978-1-945102-50-9

9 781945 102509

Snakes & Ladders or Vice Versa

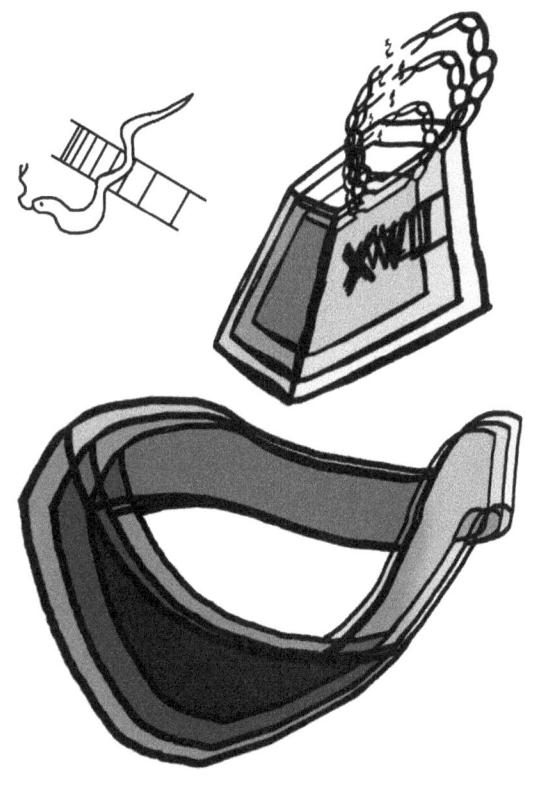

Riley Maiden

"If anyone ever attacks you with a raspberry, simply pull the lever and a 16-ton weight will drop on his head."

Monty Python's Flying Circus, S1E4,
"Owl-Stretching Time"

Sorry about this one. It gets a bit silly.

Archie Boaconstrictor (one word) was a merry old man, despite being only twenty-six and in actuality rather young. Additionally, he was perpetually unhappy, rendering him not quite as merry as some people would have you believe.

As a fairly young man trapped like a fly in amber in the modern age of time—to put it simply, the present—he naturally had numerous grievances with the UK and, more specifically, the world around him, chief of which being the fact that everything in the entire world (no exceptions!) was all-around horrible, terrible, appalling, and above all unredeemable. And this was barely scratching the surface! It was really quite sensible grounds for deep-seated misanthropy, or so he figured. To that end, he mainly spent his days staring blankly at the television, the coffee table, or both simultaneously, if he could manage it.

His wife of two or so years, Emma Ballpython (also one word)—a ball python—very often disagreed with her husband's outlook. She deduced that Archie's radical viewpoints ultimately stemmed from his disgust and disillusionment with the human race—which is, of course, the definition of misanthropy—but also, she found, his disgust with himself for having the gall to be part of it. As a ball python, though, Emma didn't have that problem. Maybe that's why he married her.

One night, Emma wrapped herself around Archie's neck, as she did most nights.

"Look, Archie," Emma said, "I really do think you've got everything all wrong."

"Oh, rubbish," Archie scowled. "What do you know, then? You're not even bloody human."

"Well, I'd think that's hardly the point!" she exclaimed. "Really, Archie. Even *you* must recognize the undeniable presence of good throughout the world."

"Now that's just silly," he scoffed. "I tell you, woman, this country—no, this *planet*—is run by a bunch of bloody *snakes!*"

Emma glared at Archie, considerably.

"Ah. Well... you bloody well know what I mean, Emma!"

This conversation repeated very nearly almost every other night, near-verbatim. Archie was quite stubbornly set in his ways, Emma found—but she, in turn, was stubbornly set on doing away with her husband's attitude. She simply had to find the means to do so.

Luckily, she was in luck. It was nearing Christmas time, and Archie and Emma, despite their innumerable disagreements, always had a mutual love for Christmas time. It was the one time of year where Archie would open up his heart a little, and maybe even begin to consider the otherwise absurd notion that the human race may not be all that bad. Emma had to work quickly, though; the minute Christmas time was over, Archie would simply revert right back to his old self, much to the chagrin and annoyance of everyone around him.

Something decidedly sinister was brewing in the bowels of the UK government, however. This seemed to be common practice for the UK government, though, so most people had gone to become apathetic or indifferent. Most of the government's schemes were either too silly, too contrived, or simply too elaborate to go anywhere, anyway, so what did anyone care? It wasn't like this new scheme would end up any differently.

Enter the newly-appointed Prime Minister—the Slight Honourable Oliver Cobra (also one word), who was a cobra, was currently overseeing the current scheme. As the current leader of the Conservative Party, he had managed to convince—or, more accurately, "convince"—nearly everyone on his side of Parliament that Christmas ought to be outlawed and was now hoping to work on "convincing" the Opposition.

"If you're like me," Cobra announced, "then you ought to know just how problematic Christmas is. Just think of those who practise other religions. Wouldn't want them left out, now would we? Now *would we?*"

"Ah, but, sir," one dissenter dissented, "many other religions have their own holidays in place of or in addition to Christmas, sir. Why specifically target Christmas, then?"

Cobra glared at the dissenter, considerably.

"Furthermore," another dissenter joined in, "Christmas isn't necessarily mutually exclusive to the many forms of Christianity. A friend of mine's Jewish, and her family celebrates Christmas as well… if only for the presents, and the fact that all her neighbours and friends celebrate Christmas."

Cobra was forced to glare cockeyed in order to glare at both of them.

"And I'd just like to point out," the previous dissenter continued dissenting, "that the vast majority of the UK celebrates Christmas. In addition, outlawing it on religious grounds breaches the clause of freedom of religious expression. It's *illegal* to ban Christmas, sir."

"It's great for the British economy, too, sir," the other dissenter added.

Cobra lessened his glare as he deliberated, contemplated, and otherwise pretended to consider the dissenters' arguments. After a few moments, he turned back to them.

"You both raise excellent points, gentlemen," Cobra grinned. "But I'm afraid I'm going to have to kill the both of you."

Cobra prepared to arm himself with his hunting six-shooter, but he could not do so due to his distinct lack of arms. He resolved, then, to push the large and imposing red button on his desk, dropping sixteen-ton weights on both of the dissenters simultaneously.

"Right-o," Cobra calmly exclaimed. "Would anyone else like to weigh in?"

"Personally, I don't think the Prime Minister should be allowed to have sixteen-ton weights in the first place," Archie groaned, staring at the television as he snacked on a bag of crisps. "Bloody Tory snakes, thinking they run the bloody country."

"Did you even see the broadcast, Archie?" Emma cried. "The government wants to *ban* Christmas! That's deplorable! They can't just ban Christmas anytime they like."

"Mind you, Emma," Archie continued, finishing the last of his bag, "I'll bet the bloody Opposition is raring to get their hands on some sixteen-ton weights. Bloody Labour snakes, thinking they run the bloody country."

Emma hissed aggravatingly at her husband. "Listen to me! They want to *ban. Christmas.* I don't know if there's even a referendum! That Oliver Cobra's nothing but bad news."

"Nothing that can be done about it, Emma," Archie insisted. "If they're going to ban Christmas, then they're going to ban Christmas. What's the use of worrying?"

Despite her husband's nonchalance, Emma grew quite worried. Christmas time was swiftly approaching—faster than a jet-propelled cheetah—and if it were to be outlawed, Archie would never think to pour his heart out to her, and that simply would not do. Then again, Emma doubted he would have the gall to pour his heart out anyway, being an Englishman, but that was beside the point. Regardless, she knew what she had to do. And, she had to do it rather quickly.

"Right, Archie, I'll tell you what," Emma proposed. "You know my grandfather, the Lord Ballpyhton?[1] He has considerable influence, you know. I'll bet you a shilling we can do away with this Christmas ban by teatime."

"Well, that makes me a shilling richer," Archie smirked. "You've got yourself a bet."

Archie extended his arm to shake on it, momentarily confusing Emma. She saw the gesture as an invitation to wrap herself around his forearm, which she did.

"Right. I say let's be off," Emma exclaimed. "Lord Ballpyhton has a house in the country, so we'll have to make our way there."

"*We?* But there's Football on the telly..."

Archie pointed to the Football that he had placed on top of the television set.

"Football's *always* on the telly," Emma hissed. "You can watch it anytime. Let's go!"

Emma proverbially dragged her husband to his car in order to drive to the train station, which brought them to the country, which brought them to a field of poppies, barley, and cacti. After traversing the poppy, barley, and cactus field, they eventually made their way to Lord Ballpyhton's cottage—Battersea Power Station—which is where they hoped to end up all along.

---

[1] This is the correct spelling.

"I've been meaning to ask," Archie meant to ask. "Why's your grandfather's name spelled like that? It should be Lord *Ballpython*, not *Ballpyhton*. Shouldn't it?"[2]

"Well," Emma explained, "he was originally Montgomery Anaconda-Gartersnake-Ballpython. When he became a Lord, he wanted to shorten it to just Lord Ballpython, but he spelled it wrong."

"*He* spelled it wrong?"

"Yeah. He wrote 'Lord Pallbyhton.' They went to correct it, but they ended up spelling it 'Ballpyhton' instead. Nobody bothered to correct it a second time."[3]

"See, that's what you get when you let a bunch of bleedin' *snakes* run the bleedin' House of Lords," Archie grumbled.

Emma glared at him, considerably.

"Ah. Well, you know what I mean, Emma."

Entering the power station-cottage, Emma and Archie sniffed around in search of the Lord Ballpyhton. They made particular note of the dimmed lights and overall absence of sound, activity, and life in general, which was ample cause for suspicion.

"Granddad?" Emma called out. "It's Emma and Archie. Are you home?"

Emma thought she heard a bit of rustling coming from upstairs. Additionally, she also thought she heard a thundering crash that reverberated throughout the cottage.

"What on earth was that?" Archie whispered.

---

[2] Despite Archie's inclination to believe otherwise, "Ballpyhton" is still the correct spelling.

[3] This affirms that "Ballpyhton" is indeed the correct spelling.

"I thought I heard something, yeah," Emma softly replied. "Let's go check it out."

As the couple made their way upstairs, they found themselves rather jarred by the bleak darkness enveloping the hall; strangely, it seemed to grow progressively darker as they neared the Lord Ballpyhton's chambers. Emma thought she had adequate night vision, but wasn't quite sure. Archie, of course, was right out of luck in that regard, though Emma was nonetheless able to steer her husband in their desired direction. Opening the Lord Ballpyhton's chamber, the lights, all at once, suddenly flashed on, momentarily blinding everybody in the room. Once Archie and Emma regained their sight, they found the Lord Ballpyhton incapacitated underneath a sixteen-ton weight.

"Emma, my dear, is that you?" the Lord Ballpyhton called out. "Thank God you're here. I've been crushed under this sixteen-ton weight."

"Yes, Granddad," Emma replied, "I've noticed."

The Lord turned to Archie. "And you've brought your wife—er, husband—along, too, I see! Wonderful to see you again, old bean. How are things with you these days?"

"Dreadful," Archie scowled.

"Nothing's changed with you, I see," the Lord laughed. "Anyway, I'd love to chat, but as you can see, I'm in a bit of a pickle at the moment. The new Prime Minister—that Oliver Cobra fellow—has been trying to kill me for weeks!"

"I can't imagine why," Emma replied, with sincere sincerity.

"Well, you know, Emma, my dear, I may be Conservative, but that Cobra twit has always gotten under my scales. Never liked him. Not once. Excuse me..."

The Lord turned away to cough, considerably.

"...Anyway, I've been an outspoken critic of his policies and schemes ever since he was appointed. Especially this new one about outlawing Christmas! Isn't that just silly? Anyway, Cobra doesn't like dissent, so he dropped a sixteen-ton weight on me."

"Sounds fun," Archie snidely remarked.

"Quite so, old chap," the Lord replied. "There's one thing he didn't count on, though. Back in my day, see, I was in the Army! I was expertly trained in the art of defence against sixteen-ton weights. Couldn't tell you just how many times it's saved my life."

"So, where's Cobra gone now?" Emma questioned.

"I'd wager the bugger's on his way back to London, my dear," the Lord answered. "He's planning on making a speech in Parliament, which is when he'll formally outlaw Christmas. If you're going after him, you ought to hurry, and rather quickly, too. Win one for me, will you?"

"Speaking of wagers," Archie reminded Emma, "it's past teatime."

"Oh, bugger," Emma scoffed. She handed him a shilling.

After reverse-traversing the cacti, barley, and poppy fields, Archie and Emma made their way back to the train station, from which they hopped back in Archie's car in order to drive to the nearest Tube station, which eventually brought them to Central London. While making their way to Parliament, they began to notice increasing amounts of anti-Christmas propaganda from both the Tories and Labour (Emma speculated that Cobra was able to drop some weights on the Opposition), ranging from standard posters containing silly reasons for why Christmas ought to be banned forever to more aggressive billboards declaring that Father Christmas is a home invader and a felon, and he would be arrested on sight if they could only track the bugger down.

"I haven't seen this much bloody propaganda since the last time I saw this much bloody propaganda," Archie grumbled. "It's all the bloody same, it is."

"Good on them for putting on a show, though," Emma remarked. "At least they're *pretending* to give us a choice in the matter."

Archie and Emma did eventually make it to the Palace of Westminster, though, which is where they ultimately wanted to end up all along. Opening the door, they came across a security guard, whom they knew was a security guard as he had "A SECURITY GUARD" written on his uniform.

"Ah, excuse us, sir," Emma began asking the guard, "but can you point us to Parliament?"

The guard narrowed his eyes and raised his right brow. "You're *in* Parliament, ma'am."

"We're, ah, not *in* Parliament, sir," she corrected him, shaking her head. "We're just ordinary British citizens, we are."

"Right, sorry. My bad, ma'am," the guard apologised.

"Anyway, we were hoping to catch the Prime Minister," Emma continued. "We heard he would be coming here today."

"Yes, of course. Last I heard, he was making his way to the House of Lords..."

As the guard was speaking, a cacophony of syncopated, thundering crashes came from the general direction of the House of Lords.

"...Well, never mind, ma'am," the guard said, "I think he's just finished there. He should be heading to Commons next, then."

Emma shook her head once again. "Can you give us directions?"

"Of course, ma'am. There are a number of directions, among them north, south, east, and..."

"No, no. I meant directions to the House of Commons," Emma corrected him.

"Right. Sorry, ma'am. Head up those stairs, third door on your left."

Luckily, Emma and Archie were both quite adept at following directions and at some point found their way to the House of Commons. Upon entering the room, they were greeted by a mass congregation of MPs—half of them hissing heartily, the other reluctantly hissing heartily out of fear of having something dropped onto them—as the Prime Minister Cobra prepared to prepare his speech.

"Now, tell me," Cobra began, "are there any champions of Christmas in the room this evening? If there are, I ask that you please raise your hand."

The MPs looked around at each other, puzzled. Being snakes, none of them had hands.

"Splendid," Cobra grinned. "Now, I take that to mean we all agree on the outlawing of Christmas? If so, I ask that you please make yourselves known... by raising your hand."

As expected, none of the MPs were able to procure the necessary appendages for the act of hand-raising and thus were unable to do so.

"I see," Cobra lamented. "I sincerely appreciate your thoughts. However, I'm afraid I simply cannot tolerate any opposition. Ta."

As Cobra prepared himself to make snake oil of the MPs, Archie and Emma, watching from the sidelines, mutually agreed that enough was enough and, seeing how the present moment was the perfect opportunity to do away with the Prime Minister, decided to just get on with it.

"I've got a plan, Emma," Archie whispered. "Listen—if we circle around and taunt him enough, we'll be able to change places and drop a weight on him. Nice and karmic."

"Actually, Archie, I was thinking," Emma responded, "we should just have a chat with him or something. Make him see the error of his ways in a decidedly Christmas-y fashion. Your idea's really silly and far-fetched, anyway."

Archie narrowed his eyes. "Look here, woman. Can you really blame me? I can't think of anything that's bloody clever enough."

Emma glared at him, considerably. "It doesn't necessarily have to be clever, you know. It's just got to be able to work."

"Tell you what," Archie began proposing, "why don't we follow my plan—circle around, switch places, drop the weight on him—but instead of taunting him, you can chat with him and try to get him to see how wonderful Christmas time is. Then, we'll drop it on him."

"Right then, fine. I suppose that works."

Putting their plan into action, Archie and Emma shouted in Cobra's general direction in order to get his attention, from which they proceeded to circle around him.

"Who in blazes are you two?" Cobra hissed. "And what in God's name are you doing trespassing in Parliament?"

"We're petitioners," Emma replied, "and we're petitioning."

As Archie suspected, they were all beginning to switch places.

"Wait a tic," Cobra questioned. "Aren't you the Lord Ballpyhton's[4] granddaughter? What a sly little twit he was. I suppose you won't be any different, will you?"

---

[4] Even Oliver Cobra, the bad guy, knows this is the correct spelling.

Emma began glaring a bit. "Not necessarily, if you're willing to listen to reason."

"Not really. But I am enjoying this circling-around thing."

Cobra and Emma began a back-and-forth rapport, detailing in detail how Christmas ought to be banned and why it's the silliest thing she's ever heard, respectively. Archie, meanwhile, was fully invested in getting everyone to switch places, which seemed to be working. In fact, it was. Once Cobra was in position, Archie, promptly and with very little hesitation, pulled the PM's button and flicked his lever, thus dropping a sixteen-ton weight on him. The MPs were too dazed and confused to issue a proper response and were far more concerned with who among them would get to be Prime Minister next.

"Well, you know, that Lord Ballpyhton's a decent chap," suggested one Tory MP. "Why not let him be the Prime Minister?"

"Because he's a bloody Tory, that's why!" a Labour MP shouted out. "He'll just bring us right back to where we are now, with this silly outlawing of Christmas. Besides, he's a Lord."

"Ah, well... I've never been Prime Minister before, you know," mumbled another MP. "I was thinking maybe I could have a go. I won't outlaw Christmas, honest."

Archie shook his head. "Typical, really. That's all these bloody Parliament snakes do. They argue and argue and argue, but they never get anything done, do they?"

Emma glared at him, considerably.

"Listen, Emma. You know I'm right this time."

The next morning, nearly everyone in government had uncharacteristically come to a consensus and decided that the Lord Ballpyhton should be the next Prime Minister and lead the Conservative Party. Being a Lord, though, it was ultimately agreed that him being Prime Minister was not a very good idea, and as such settled for his son and Emma's father, Andrew Anaconda-Gartersnake-Ballpython, a Tory backbencher, next in line for the head of the Conservative Party, and decidedly not a Lord. Once in office, he shortened his name to simply Andy Ballpython to save time and did away with his predecessor's plans to outlaw Christmas to save headache.

Noticing an outcry from certain loud and annoying minority groups across Britain, though, the new Prime Minister ultimately and begrudgingly decided to hold a referendum. Some groups argued that Christmas had become far too commercialized and had lost its meaning, citing the countless Christmas-themed songs, films, and short story compilation books; some others asserted that it was a cornerstone of the oppressive status quo and was due for a good abolishing; many others were simply tired of going through the motions of buying presents every year. In the end, though, the majority of the UK decided they really quite enjoyed Christmas and would like to keep it around for the time being. Archie, upon hearing the results, became quite happy for once.

"Well, would you look at that?" Archie grinned. "I suppose most people have some good sense in them after all."

"I'm glad you've finally coming around," Emma smiled.

"I mean," Archie continued, "it doesn't excuse the love and glorification of war and violence, widespread terrorism, global corruption, continued apathy towards numerous worldwide issues, the general air of complacency, and those bloody rapid-fire hi-hats on every new song nowadays..."

Emma glared at him, considerably.

"Ah. But you know what? I suppose I can forgive them for now."

About the Author

Riley Maiden is a college student, musician, hobbyist animator, cat-petting enthusiast, and staunch Oxford comma supporter who can now add "published author" to his list of fictitious credentials. He was born in California some years ago on the 28th of April and has been acting dangerously silly ever since. In high school, he dabbled in theatre, choir, and team-based improv before graduating and thereby losing regular access to such things. As a music-lover, some of his favorite musical artists include the likes of Genesis, King Crimson, and David Bowie, and his favorite album by the Jimi Hendrix Experience is more or less Axis: Bold as Love. He hopes to eventually pursue music full-time, but he recognizes the overall improbability of such a thing happening and, as such, is also pursuing a degree in history.

The Person I See in the Mirror

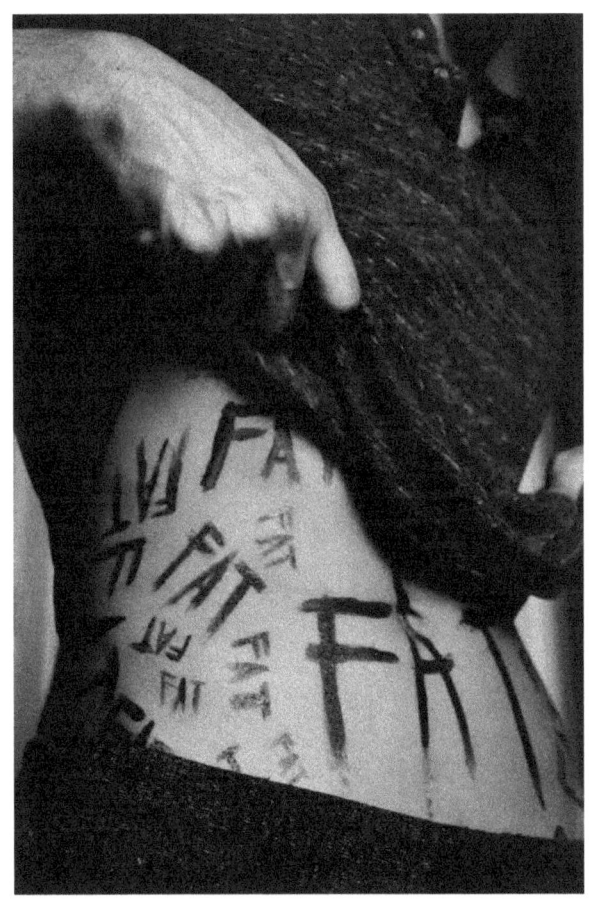

Julian Martinez

"If you can't fly then run, if you can't run then walk, if you can't walk then crawl, but whatever you do, you have to keep moving forward."

Martin Luther King, Jr.

At exactly 5:00 AM, the obnoxious, repulsive, and thundering siren that was the default iPhone "radar alarm" echoed across the barren tile flooring of my house. The alarm was distinctly recognizable as the noise shattered the lull reticence that encapsulated the thin bordering walls. A moment passed, and the room was silent, yet the roaring sound resonated, lingering with a feeling of remembrance, knowing that it would go off soon again.

With my eyes barely peering open, I was greeted with the radiant light of my phone screen illuminating the dismal bleakness of my room which was otherwise boarded up in darkness. As I struggled to read the blinding screen of my phone alongside the contrast of the dark room, the temptation to simply close my lethargic eyes grew increasingly more enticing. "Thursday, 5:03 AM."

Sluggishly, I browsed through the YouTube library, listening to music and fighting the longing urge to lull back into a sleep, until I eventually made the forceful decision to pick myself up and prepare for the day.

I stumbled to the dresser across the room and pulled open the top drawer which held an army of socks and underwear, randomly chose a pair, and then continued to the second drawer. To the left of the drawer was a stack of hellish "attention seekers" otherwise known as short-sleeved shirts, which were typically unworn outside of the comfort of my room. Wearing short-sleeved shirts was a tedious and complicated process, which was especially difficult for me. Take a moment and search into Google, "People wearing short-sleeved shirts," only to be hit with a barrage of muscular middle-aged men.

There was an obvious demographic. My body, however, was best comparable to a skeleton bonded together with a thin layer of skin and flesh that was only further accentuated from wearing short sleeves. My lack of comfort in wearing these shirts led me to stray away from this particular article of clothing in exchange for the comfort of baggier hoodies and sweats. Alternatively, to short-sleeved shirts, the drawer was filled with a stack of flannels as well as my overbearing collection of hoodies, which were both safer options in comparison to the dreadful thought of wearing short-sleeved shirts. After a moment of debate, I grabbed a black school hoodie and moved to the third drawer, which held an array of different sweatpants making it easy for me to simply grab a pair and proceed with the rest of my day.

Clothes in hand, I made my way to the door, struggling to keep the motivation I so desperately needed to stay awake. For a moment, I was still, standing directly in front of the door, staring at the fine wood indentations on the flat surface as I listened from the narrow crack that divided the floor and base of the door only to hear the faint voice of my mother who must have just woken up. I loved my mom. She was always a hard worker and my greatest motivation; however, she could be "difficult" in the mornings, so it was as often best to steer clear of her in order to avoid a verbal war. I hesitated as I carefully placed my hand on the cold metal of the door handle, slowly turning it with an uttermost level of control until it met with the resistance of the door. I was cautious as I pulled the handle towards myself, trying my best to minimize the high-pitched creeks of the turning door. Presently, I was slow as I took my initial step out of the room in order to assure a level of discrepancy, but then I quickly hurried across the hall towards the restroom.

In a quick motion, the bathroom door swung open and then closed again. Immediately, I turned on the fan and took a breath of relief. The room was still, and the fan provided just the right amount of white noise that held a generous degree of privacy. I briefly paused taking a moment to collect myself before I looked up, panning the room, noticing the shower, and then the picture on the wall, and finally pausing at the toilet that sat in the corner of the room, just for a second.

I took a step towards the mirror staring at my reflection, noticing my disgusting and rather gaudy morning appearance. I nodded at myself as a method of reassurance yet still stood in disbelief knowing that though today was seemingly starting off highly, it would soon crash into a shitshow, or so that's typically the pattern of the deaf days that so often kept me booked. I walked to the shower to then grab the metal handle, pushing it ever so slightly, just enough to contend for a light stream of running water. This was presently the lowest setting the shower could be set, the coldest for that matter. Cold showers weren't always pleasant; however, they were more effective than an obnoxious alarm clock sounding off at 5 AM. While I had become accustomed to the glacial shock of a routinely cold shower, the uncomfortable and rather agonizing process never became less tortuous.

As I stood there, waiting on the mat placed directly outside of the shower, I felt the icicle like sprites of water pierce my skin preparing me for the sheer cold avalanche of liquid that awaited me. After a few moments of hesitation and a period of wavering commitment, I all at once took an aggressive and forced step forward that led me directly under the stream of hell that pierced my soul. Though the initial shock of a cold shower was unpleasant, I was often surprised by the comfort I found. After a moment of hell, it was relieving; it was comforting despite the process it took to get there. For one reason or another, the cold water kept me happy or maybe more so content; if anything, it was an incredible place to think. All in all, it kept me sane.

Promptly concluding my five-minute torture ritual, I shut off the water and opened the door to then immediately grasp the heavenly warmth of the nearest towel and quickly dried off. After putting on my clothes, I then brushed my teeth, flossed, and put on deodorant until I felt I was at a level of presentability. I stared myself down in the mirror one last time and muttered, "Today is going to be a good day." I turned around, clutched the handle of the door, and made my way back to my room.

There was only a sliver of dim light that protruded from underneath the closed curtains hanging on the wall, it was still early. I opened my phone to see the digital numbers on the screen read, "Tuesday, 6:15 AM." I had about an hour before Skye would be at my house to pick me up for school, so I quickly made my bed and hid the mess around my room to a satisfaction that justified lying around and listening to Pandora.

My eyes creaked open, just slightly as the light irritated the stillness of my face. For just a moment, the room was still, but then with a deep and piercing alarm, I forced my eyes open, realizing I had fallen asleep. Immediately, I rummaged through the cloud-like texture of my bed searching for my phone, which had rendered itself lost as I worried that Skye had already arrived and had been kept waiting. After what felt like ages, I had my phone in a death grip of my hand. The screen taunted me as I was greeted with, "Low Battery: 20% Battery Remaining," which now had to be sustained for the entirety of my day. To my surprise, my phone remained dead silent, absent of other messages or notifications; however, my concern now was that Skye failed to wake up. Rushingly, I collected myself and continued to gather my daily necessities as I longed for a message. Eventually, the clock hit 7:40. Still with no response, I opened my messages with a back and forth debate of calling until finally the phone vibrated. My soul sighed to the feeling of relief as I read that she was on her way.

Three or so minutes passed as I refreshed my Snapchat notifications maybe every 5 to 10 seconds, waiting for a response until finally, there was the exciting vibration of the phone that followed up with a notification reading, "Skye is typing." I didn't need to read the message; I knew she was here, so I casually sauntered outside and jumped in her car. The drive felt typical, ordinary. It was routine that I was updated on the recent antsy gossip. It was truthfully shocking, or at least for me it was, as I was often known to maintain a towering defense preserving my raw feelings, which left drowning in a state of incredulity. What differentiated her from the rest was that Skye was always caring and was never seen dismissing someone's feelings in light of another opinion despite the believability or lack thereof. Being alongside Skye was simply amazing, not only because of the convenience of the ride, but also because she was one of the reasons I was kept sane through my shitshow of a life. She didn't think I was crazy, but then again there weren't things I left to question due to my careful and considerate planning of how I chose my words. Mayhaps, it was for the best to leave a bit of wonder to life, who knows.

We eventually creeped forward towards the entrance of the school where the parking lots grazed ahead. Due to our apparent yet predictable lateness, parking was always a gamble; however, we continued to drive up to the nearest parking area where we snaked through the rows rushingly praying for a spot.

Truthfully, I was in shock that we hadn't been dropped from the class or lectured as we had not once been on time this semester. Personally, we had this unspoken consensus that our professor liked us for who knows what reason and had at times used that as our personal excuse in order to alleviate a bit of stress or maybe to just excuse our embarrassment whenever we walked in the room.

Skye and I rushed our way to the classroom, using fear as our speed boost where we arrived outside the door a lucky eight minutes late, which was actually better than usual. The handle gleamed as I stood there recalling the dreadful fear in opening the door. It was never a pleasant experience as the room was always left in a sheer silence. If someone were to drop a pen, the impact on the floor would resonate for just about the next five minutes, let alone making a mid-class entrance jutting open the old, clangy, metal door. It was generally a mix of an awkward and embarrassing shame as the eyes of the room swung from a hypnotized attention to then darting at us as we held our heads down quickly scrambling to arrive at a seat.

Class went by extremely fast and relievingly so. Throughout the entire hour-long session, my stomach tantrumed and screamed with groans of hunger. It was embarrassing, but I couldn't dismiss the fact that it was at fault as this was a result of my obvious lack of eating. I often refused to eat breakfast in the mornings because the thought of food immediately after waking up was repulsive, though I typically wouldn't give this much thought because it was recurrent and customary to fast throughout the day to then compensate later on when I got home. This was usually perfect because I would have around twenty minutes to pillage around the kitchen prior to the rest of my family coming home.

Aside from my beauty pageant standard starvation period, the rest of my day was fairly simple and straightforward primarily because the remainder of my daily classes had been canceled leaving me with the most vigorous task of finding a place to wait in boredom while Skye's classes ended. During this time, I habitually walked around campus until my stomach was naturally lured to the temptations of the student store.

Walking through the aisles, I often spent an exponential amount of time looking at things that I didn't necessarily need yet passed the time. In order to avoid the blank stares of employees, I always put in my earbuds and played it as though I was receiving a call. I spent some time skimming the aisles for some snack to soothe the wailing beast that was my stomach, but there was an obvious problem that constantly presented itself with nearly every treat on the board. The initial thought of chips or cookie-like crackers was extremely tempting, but think about the fat, the sugar, the edible junk that I would be shoveling into my body. Beef Jerky was grossly dried, and the thought of a pulverized cow wasn't all that exciting. Knowing the importance of eating lunch and maintaining a level of sanity throughout the day, I settled for a bright green package of chewing gum.

Promptly after making the exchange, I undressed the plastic wrapping that encapsulated gum, popped open the paper seal, and threw a piece of minty gum in my mouth.

After finding a place to sit, I unlocked my phone and opened an app called "Daily Calorie Tracking." The app was actually a work of genius; it helped monitor daily calorie intake as well as a number of other percentages found on the back of other foods. After a quick aim and a simple scan across a barcode of the packaging of whatever food you wanted to eat, the app would automatically calculate and input different statistics that measured proper daily intake for one's target weight.

I placed my phone over the scanner on the back of the package and instantly "Wrigley's Doublemint Gum" appeared on my screen. I manually imputed "1 piece" for the serving size and was done. It was like magic.

A moment of stillness passed when my phone once again screamed and tantrumed, alarming me that Skye would soon be out of class. Making my way back to the car, I thought about my day, the interactions I made, and the lack of productivity that I was often presented with throughout my day. Nonetheless, it was Thursday, and I would soon be home.

Driving home came fast with the naked streets that were prematurely lifeless from the wavering school traffic, which was surprisingly all but apparent. My reflection mocked me as I stared out the car window, patiently waiting for the event that would doubtlessly alter the general outcome of my day. It was odd; today was fine, yet at the same time difficult and depriving. It seemed obvious or at least obvious to me, yet the silence on her lips said otherwise. The fault was mine, as I was never one to speak bluntly and forward about my feelings. Nevertheless, my house waited in the distance, as it grew taller and now stood tall over the car, as we pulled up to the driveway.

The door was towering as the reflection of the stalkerish security camera raced down, casting a gleaming light across the metal screen. For a moment, I admired the symmetrical pattern of holes and filigree that carpeted the first layer of protection to the deceiving building. After drifting into a passerby state of stillness for just a second longer, I reached back to feel the side of my bag where my house keys resided. Searching the lanyard, I came to a halt at a key with a squared backing that reluctantly begged to open the door. With my hand now placed firmly on the heavy steel grip, I choked the handle and hauled the door open, revealing the open house of which I was then resolved to welcoming myself in.

Almost instinctively, I walked towards the restroom directly to the right of the front door. The door swung open and then closed with a soft slam of the handle. At first, the room was silent and then instantly filled with the breezing noise of the fan where I stood overlooking the sink confronting the person in the mirror. Inhaling I closed my eyes, exhaled and shut off the fan and the bathroom light. I took a moment and then stepped out closing the bathroom door in front of me.

I struggled to walk towards the kitchen as I convinced myself I was nothing more than exhausted. Arriving at the pantry, I grabbed an unopened loaf of bread, the peanut butter, a Nutella spread, and a knife then retreated to the comfort of my room opening and then slamming closed the wooden door.

I felt guilty as my face fell becoming mesmerized and enthralled, as I twisted the small metal lock attached to the door, listening to the ring of the almost silent click that secluded me from the rest of the world. Turning around, I placed my back against the door to then slide down until I reached the floor. It was disgusting and selfish and even more so heartbreaking as I eyed the plastic bag that held the bread. The silence of the room was broken with the soft sound of my hand sinfully forcing as much of the delicious and soft and filling ailment into my mouth as humanly possible. It was glutinous and repulsive, purely reprehensible.

Standing up, I turned towards the door and walked towards the restroom, once again quickly opening and closing the door behind me and turning on the fan. Panning the room, I stared at the showerhead and the picture and the toilet. I stared at myself in the mirror. I looked at myself and muttered, "One time, only one more time, I promise," as I nodded in reassurance. Slowly, I kneeled down on the cold tile floor, placing one hand beside me holding myself up and the other on the rim of the toilet. The face of piggish ridicule disappeared, as the tears descended from my eyes to the water below, creating ripples that killed the reflection across the water. One last time, I stared, encapsulated by my swirling wishing well as I muttered the words, "One last time."

About the Author

Julian Martinez currently attends Crafton Hills College, aspiring a degree in Music Education and Performance. Julian has an extensive background in music spanning over a decade of which he works towards attaining a professional level of musicianship. Education has played an exponential role in Julian's gravitation towards a future in music-oriented instruction. Recognizing continual stigmatization of mental illness and self-image, Julian pushes to explore perspectives often disregarded lacking concrete understandings. Julian has often discussed the extremes of mental disorders in detail of biological and psychological intensities in hopes to bring light towards often neglected social topics.

Script

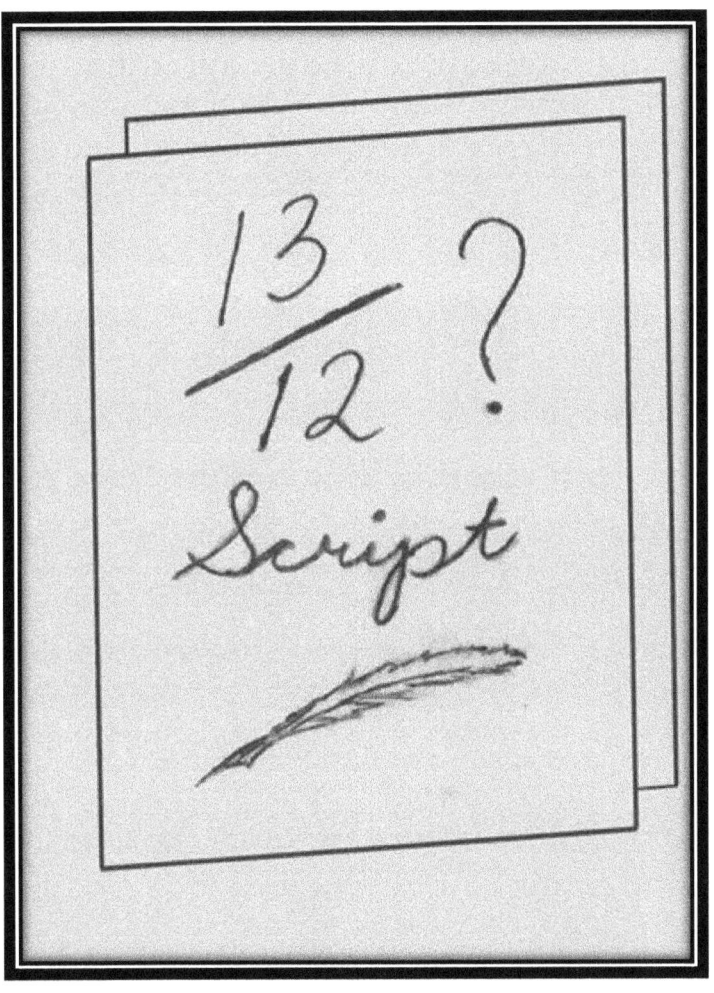

Maria Olekh

"Stories should always be told; every story has something to be learned from it, and by hearing them—by really listening—we learn to understand the people and things around us a little more and a little bit better. That's why when someone has a story they want to share, they absolutely should—and we should listen."

Maria Olekh

"So." Mother stood by the stove, cooking dinner at six-thirty in the evening as usual. "It's September, so you know what that means, right?"

Indeed.

Every September, we start preparing for the end of the year. The end of the year means hosting an event for our community of immigrants, including games, competitions, jokes, food, and even a small play for the younger children. Now, this originally started out as a small affair, but somehow, word spread, and we had to accommodate for the increase in numbers. To be a little more specific, we started out with maybe forty-fifty close friends, including their families. Now, there are more than two hundred interested in attending.

No pressure.

Now, part of the reason the event became such a big deal was because most of the event was targeted at younger children. It allowed everyone to dress up and have fun: The children got to play together while allowing the adults to relax a little.

Organizing the event itself takes about a month total, including looking for and renting out a hall for an evening, selling tickets (sponsoring an event like this is rather expensive, but the price of tickets offsets that, so really, the attendees are the ones financing the event; none of the organizers or actors are paid), among other, more minor details.

The play, on the other hand, requires much more work. First, we come up with a story (usually—who am I kidding? It's *always* my mother and me). Because it's meant for the end of the year, it's New Years' themed, meaning two of the characters have to be (our equivalent of) Santa Claus and his granddaughter. Similarly, they have to encounter some sort of New Years' themed problem—the presents go missing, or maybe the magical staff is stolen by the antagonist— really, anything works, as long as it's something the children can help fix. Oh, that's right! The play is always interactive with the children— they sing songs with and for the characters and play games, solve riddles, and "help" the actors resolve the issues. It's always important to consider what they will enjoy: which games are fun, which puzzles are just the right amount of challenging, and so on. That part's always really fun to consider.

Within the last three or four years, we also decided to try having a person in charge of sound effects and music during the performance— including fun music for the games, naturally! And, just as naturally, that responsibility *gently* fell onto my shoulders (please note the sarcasm). Jokes aside, it's always exciting to think about and pick out which goofy themes will make people smile and fit that year's play.

Another sort of fun twist that we add to each play is that we refer to the coming year's Chinese Zodiac and choose a story with an animal that matches, then rewrite it to suit our needs. This coming year's Zodiac will be the year of the Rat. Hmmm... Not much we can do with that... Good news is that it'll also be a leap year! That means more material to work with.

A while ago, we came across a parody of the twelve months, where each of the original names was changed into something similar-sounding while also poking fun at it. For example, December turned into Freezember, or September became Snotember (as representative of the beginning of flu season).

Each of the months was renamed in this way, so we thought, *Why don't we make this a part of our script?* From there, we decided to include a thirteenth month—Simpleton—who wants to join the calendar year, but isn't quite intelligent enough, nor is he very good at magic—a must for "Santa's" helpers.

There's the conflict for this year's play! Simpleton would want to become a part of the calendar year, and in his attempts to do so, he would accidentally transform the regular months into their "demented" versions! Perfect!

Well... not really, at least, not for the characters.

With a conflict in mind, we set to writing the script.

` So, September came and went, and we were nearing the middle of October. Most of the preparations were going smoothly: We were scouting out a bigger hall to rent, the presents for the children were ordered, and costumes were being made.

Just one tiny problem: We were still stuck on Scene 2 of the planned five. The general actions were planned, the outcomes were thought out, but "WHERE IS THE DIALOGUE??"

So. We had characters. We had costumes. We didn't have dialogue. That wasn't good.

Dialogue aside, we also needed to find people willing to volunteer to act in the play. So many dilemmas...

Halloween was just around the corner.

Most of the costumes were done by that point, and we had almost all of the actors. Finally, dialogue! It was written but not rehearsed. A little less than two months left... Time was running out.

Other than that, preparations were still going relatively smoothly: Presents were supposed to arrive within the first week of November, and we found enough volunteers to help make sure the event went off without a hitch.

That meant that those people would be helping set up before the event, stay after to help with cleanup, help manage the potluck, check tickets, and many other jobs. (Unfortunately, they all see my mother as an authority figure, and consequently, when something goes wrong—which it will; something *always* goes wrong—they will immediately start pestering her, or me, asking for her).

One other major problem came up; the hall that worked nicely for us last year was not available for us to use this year...! Eek!

My workload was also becoming somewhat ridiculous; on top of school and my other extracurriculars, picking out child-friendly songs took a lot of my time. When I had the time and energy, I enjoyed it. 'This one has too much character but that one's too repetitive' or 'this song works perfectly for this type of scene!' filled my days.

And so, with renewed efforts, we moved into November. My mother's friend (whom I have an immense amount of respect for) had taken it upon herself to find a suitable hall to rent, while also taking care of her numerous children and helping us with finishing the script and rehearsing with the actors.

Surprisingly, the "casting" turned out to be pretty accurate—each of the actors could play their characters with relative ease.

Rehearsals were started, and even more time passed. Because each of us had busy schedules, we met up once or twice a week, in the evenings. My father always came home at eight in the evening, and on days we'd have rehearsals, I saw him sneak past the loud boisterous not-always-on-task group of adults. Every time, without fail, I'd say, "Hey, Dad! How was your day?"

Then, he'd shrug and do a half-wave and continue on his way. (The perks of being shy and uninvolved…)

After a while, some of the actors would notice too, and his awkward shyness turned into a running joke.

Much like how the actors had to memorize their lines, I had to learn when to turn on and off each song and sound effect. One problem arose because of it.

In the play, we wanted to have Simpleton try to cast a spell in order to become the thirteenth month in the year but have it backfire and transform the three winter months into their backwards personalities. For that particular scene, we turned off the main lights and imitated lightning flashing with a special prop, as we layered thunder sound effects over the song that played as Simpleton chanted the incantation (in rhyme form, no less!).

That was the day I learned how to really work with sound. It took my mother and me over an hour of arguing, cropping, cutting, and layering to achieve an "acceptable" version.

Upon playing it for the actress, she looked me in the eye and said, "There's no way I can pull this off." So, what did we do? That's right; we rehearsed!

One hour.

Two.

Three.

At that point, the actress was just about to give up. "Why can't we just record me saying the incantation and layer it over the audio file?"

My mother and I looked at each other—the way you do when you completely understand each other's thoughts without speaking—and said, "No, we can't do that; the timing has to be very good, which is hard to do when you record, so we have to try in person."

So, we did.

November was peacefully (hectically) coming to an end. Just about all the preparations were complete; only a few loose ends remained, and we were certain that we'd be able to tie or cut them off as needed.

Only three weeks remained until the performance, and everyone was a mix of energy, whether nervous, excited, or some combination of the two.

The days went by, sometimes crawling by, and sometimes sprinting past, but looking back, time flew all too quickly. The night of the performance was upon us.

Much like I'd anticipated, we ran into problems almost immediately; the kitchen wasn't holding up well under the (admittedly disorganized) foot traffic. But! We were prepared with volunteers!

One crisis averted, but numerous others awaited.

Upon actually starting the event with some games, we discovered that the sound was not working well. Slight correction: it wasn't working at all, if the high-pitched REEEEEE was anything to go by. After frantically rearranging some wires, this trial, too, was overcome.

That was only fifteen minutes into the four-hour-long event. Oh, dear. That was sure going to be a long night. We played the preplanned games, told each other some unplanned jokes, and each of the tables wished each other "Happy Holidays!" and so, after that, we began the play.

Thankfully, it all started without a hitch. Sure, under pressure, some of the actors forgot a word here and there, but all in all, it was progressing relatively smoothly.

Oh boy, were we wrong.

A miss here, a botched line there, and a fumbling for words kept the show moving. Sure, we had to rearrange the timeline of the plan a little, but all's well that ends well, right?

About an hour later, our chaotic mess of a show came to an end. Luckily, our mistakes were only known to us, the cast, and the audience's words were somewhat reassuring: "That was such a nice play! We look forward to coming again next year!"

Making horrified eye contact, we collectively thought, *Oh. Oh no. This isn't the end. We'll have to do the same thing next year*, just like following a looping script.

About the Author

Much like many others, Maria Olekh has a number of stories that she wants to tell. She believes that stories are a source of wonder and curiosity, and consequently, that they should absolutely be told, written down, read, and shared—not necessarily in that order. She started writing rather late—at sixteen—however, her love of words and reading have been constants throughout her life. Currently, she is working on a number of poems and wants to someday publish a novel—or three. She writes in the hopes that she will one day be able to inspire her readers and make the world just a little bit more understanding—one word at a time.

That Crimson Sand

Nathaniel Ritchey

"I am the master of my fate,
I am the captain of my soul."

-William Ernest Henley "Invictus"

There's no perfect way to react to unfavorable circumstances, especially when you're not prepared for what transpires without your prior knowledge or anticipation. When I was fourteen, I had my fair share of action: I punched three separate kids on three separate occasions during school and only got into mild trouble for one of those instances.

The first kid I ever punched at school was named Carlos, and he looked so disheveled and visibly stupid that it made my stomach heave. He looked like Little Nicky, which was fitting because he had the mental capacity comparable to someone who'd suffered head trauma. This moron who possessed a face that resembled curdled milk began throwing food into my instrument locker and started teasing me by grabbing the handle of my backpack and jerking me forward and back. I turned around, upper cutting him straight in the jaw. He bled but refused to tell on me, perhaps because he knew he'd deserved it, or maybe he was too stupid—I'd believe either one.

The second kid I punched was named Bryant. He was a skinny, extremely dark kid with a rat-like face who was often referenced as looking like a burnt corndog. More so than the others, he deserved my punishment. Bryant was a rat in more than one way; you couldn't trust him. One of my friends offered him to be included in our circle of friends, to which Bryant quickly earned the ire of my friends and me. The first thing he did wrong was simply exist in an annoying way, which is not a label anyone wants attached to them, especially in middle school. Everything he did brought him trouble. The girls hated him on account that he "flirted" with everyone (if you could call his creepy method of talking to girls "flirting"). The boys at school hated him because he talked shit to most people but was never willing to throw down.

So, on top of being a creep, he was a chicken shit coward, which reflected poorly on those who kept him in their company (us). The second thing he did wrong was "flirted" with my girl. When I say, "my girl," I don't mean she was my girlfriend; we never dated, much to my dismay, but she was still "my girl" because our circle of friends had an agreement. My best friend by the name of Angel adored a beautiful girl named Roni, so nobody made moves on Roni. My other best friend Raven was twitter pated with a girl named Julia, so nobody made moves on Julia. My girl was Alejandra- nobody made moves on Alejandra. We maintained a level of respect for one another, and it was courteous to not attempt to establish a romantic relationship with a girl that somebody else held dear to his heart. Bryant didn't follow that rule, so I politely implored him to stay away from her. When I saw him continue talking to her, I politely socked him in his mouth.

The third may or may not have been out of line- I don't know because I wasn't there. Apparently, this kid named Benjamin, a short, stout boy who resembled Violet Beauregarde in her plumped up, pear-shaped form, threw a basketball at my friend Matthew and hit him in the face before proceeding to talk shit about white people. Benjamin (allegedly) screwed the pooch twice in this (supposed) altercation. Assuming all this really happened, his first mistake was throwing a basketball at my friend's face; the second mistake was talking shit about the "pigmentally challenged" demographic, of which I am a part of. I'm not saying I assault everyone who dislike white people or have something to say about my ethnic group...however, I offer to you the possibility, that potentially, I may have, just maybe, been looking for an excuse to hit this kid. On top of being extremely annoying (more on that later), Angel had a problem with him, which to be honest, I'm not sure if it was because Benjamin talked shit to him (which I'd seen with my own eyes) or because Angel started bullying him (because as much as I love Angel, I admit he had the potential, if not a tendency, to do that). But it didn't really matter; while he was stuffing his fat, pig-like face with hot Cheetos, I decked him right in the face and cut my knuckle open on his tooth. While he was walking back to class, Angel thought it was hot Cheeto powder across his mouth, but it was blood...

Unfortunately for me, Benjamin told on me, and it wasn't hard for faculty members to find me. I was one of maybe eight white kids that went to my school, but I was one of only two with long hair, and both of us were in orchestra class during the next period, so they'd have found me no matter what. The security guard who picked me up from orchestra class ordered me to go and wash my hands at the nurse's station on account of my shredded knuckle. I saw the nurse tending to him, and I immediately felt bad, not for him, but the nurse; I had gone and made her day a lot more complicated than it needed to be. Remember how I said this kid was annoying? When the security guard accompanied me to the nurse's station to wash my knuckle, he began laughing at the kid and exclaiming, "Wow, that must have been some punch," before laughing hysterically some more. Then, his mother didn't press charges, so I assume because I may have done him some good; I'm not sure. But then, on top of those two scenarios, I met the poor kid at church a couple of months later, and what a poor sight to see that was. The youth pastors wanted nothing to do with him and visibly rolled their eyes as he approached. You know it's bad when even children of God don't want to share a roof with you on Sunday morning.

Based on my accounts, you may assume I was not necessarily an active kid when it came to fighting; you could say I was more of a punch-happy kid. If anyone felt froggy, I was the one who was leaping, not them; but the way I saw it, I was taking care of business. If anyone wanted to mess with me, no matter how big they were, how strong they were, or whatever lapse in physical attribute there was, I was still willing to fight. I was bullied by this big kid named Jeffrey who must have been about six feet tall and had the face of a shark. One day, I told him we were going to fight, and when I called him out, he was very surprised. For the most part, I was a well-respected individual, but on the occasion when somebody tried to take advantage of me or bully me without consequences, I was quick to remind them that I was willing to throw punches regardless how big and shark-like they were.

In eighth grade, however, after my grandfather passed away, I began to slow down on punching people in the face.

That's not to say I didn't stand up for myself; that's not to say there weren't still incidents few and far between where I became confrontational, but after my grandfather passed away, I was a completely different person. For the most part, those people that I battered had it coming to them, especially Carlos and Bryant. At least, that's what I believed at the time, but I was hurting, and "taking care of business" just wasn't a priority of mine; I needed to take care of myself.

I took a week off following my grandfather's passing. When I returned the following week, I found myself being dragged into trouble.

When I came back to school, it was relatively the same except the people in my class knew I had just suffered a great loss. Everything was a little quieter; questions that teachers usually directed at me were directed at others, friends I talked to were less eager to start conversations with me and waited for me to initiate them, and I was given time to just simply exist without too many distractions. I was walking down the stairs to my next classroom when my best friend, Angel, a big kid with short hair who sported glasses and a snapback, ran into me. The first thing he told me was: "Me and Rolando are going to fight!"

Some background information is needed to understand who Rolando is and how he was an important role to this story and how he had gotten himself into the role that he was playing. Among my best friends was a boy named Alfredo, a tall, fit womanizer who played soccer and participated in underage drinking. Alfredo had gotten into a fight with Rolando's best friend named Gabriel. Gabriel had been to Juvenile Hall and was gang affiliated, but beyond this I didn't know much else about him. Rolando was in the same gang that Gabriel was in, and though I don't know quite how it came to be, he and Angel, much like Alfredo and Gabriel, began to develop a mutually sustained hatred for one another.

It actually surprised me that Rolando and Angel had committed to fighting because Rolando was one of those kids like Bryant- his alligator mouth was too big for his hummingbird ass; he had a lot of fighting words, but he didn't do a lot of fighting, In one instance, my friend, Raven and I were walking to his house after school when Rolando passed us in his car and did the hand motions of a drive-by to us. The next day, I confronted him on the issue and asked him if we had a problem, but he refused to admit there was any animosity between us. From there, I labeled him a coward; I didn't understand how somebody would be willing to perform such a brazen threat and then not want to fight me. I should have kicked his ass for the disrespect alone, but at the time, I didn't consider a fact that I've considered many years later- he was probably not prepared to fight on school premises. Despite my willingness to throw down on campus, not everyone was willing to take care of business in the heat of the moment...

After announcing he was going to fight Rolando, Angel told me that he wanted me to be there on the day of the fight, which they'd planned for the next day. I lived on the opposite side of town from all my friends, but I would walk home with them to their houses fairly often, so I decided the only difference between this outing and the others was the fact that my best friend was going to fight this kid before we all hung out. So, I agreed to show up even though my better judgment told me otherwise.

That day when we were at lunch with our group of friends, we started feeling concerned about Gabriel. We concluded he wasn't the kind of person who would let his buddy and Angel fight honorably if Angel started winning, which all of us were certain was going to happen. We began to formulate a strategy in case something happened. Over the course of the lunch period, we formed a plan that we would carry out the next day.

We counted how many people we had that were going to be present for the brawl. We had Angel (obviously), me, Raven, Elijah, Andrew, our friend David, whom we called "Gay David," little Eric, along with a couple of others who aren't significant enough for me to remember. We counted about eleven who were going along with us. Alfredo volunteered himself saying that he would fight Gabriel if he stepped in. Elijah, a friend of ours whom I could only describe as "a big fucking boy with fists the size of a Christmas ham," was going to intimidate their friends with his sheer size and strength (he was considered the second strongest boy in school). Raven and I agreed that we would not jump in unless somebody else did, opting to let the two settle their dispute without getting involved if we could help it.

The details of the arranged kerfuffle were standard. We would meet at an alley (which we referred to as "The Alley") after school on Tuesday. Rolando would bring his people, and we would bring our people. All of this was fine and dandy, everything was arranged and agreed upon.

As said earlier, with most things, nobody can plan out every little detail, but we weren't worried.

While I was at home, I didn't think about the fight too much. When I did start thinking about it, I tried to push it aside... I was doubting myself.

I was always willing to fight, but the truth is I hadn't fought anyone in a long time. Nobody I ever hit swung back, and anyone I met with threats wouldn't engage me. I worried about being a liability should something happen... I did what any normal kid would do- push it off as anticipation and nervousness.

When the next day rolled around, there was a weird energy about the entire school. Nobody seemed to pay any mind to the fact that there was a fight taking place after school; everybody was cool as Joe Camel. To the credit of everybody that was involved in the fight that was to take place, everybody kept their mouths shut. A lot of times if something was going down, the whole school knew well in advance, but not this time; no outsiders were permitted to be privy to our endeavor.

I was anxious; I wanted everything to go down without a hitch. I'd been preparing by running the scenario through in my head the whole night before and in every class leading up to sixth period.

What if Gabriel tries to jump in? I thought to myself. *Alfredo has it handled; he's kicked his ass before, and he can kick his ass again. What if the cops come because somebody tipped them off? Well, at least I'm not the slowest one here. What if by some mistake Angel ends up losing the fight? Won't happen. Is anyone going to find out? Are we going to get in trouble? No way, business as usual.*

Normally when school ended, we'd make our way to our respective ladies and talk to them for a couple of minutes before going home, but today was different. We did not have the luxury of being able to waste time; we had business to get to. Angel, Raven, and I all met up together with our buddy Gay David. Elijah and Alfredo were going to walk separately but meet us there with a few more friends.

Raven, David, Angel, and I cut through the back of the school and walked out the back way, which the school greatly discouraged us from doing. My cheap, poverty-stricken school probably didn't have enough staff to make sure that the back way was secured. The back gate to the school was always locked, but there was a gap in the fence that you could jump over with little effort. Alfredo, Elijah, and the others were walking from the front of the school, which wasn't terribly far from The Alley, but you had to walk a long and winding couple of blocks to get there. My three friends and I made it to The Alley before anyone else. The Alley itself was a mixture of asphalt and sand; cars rarely drove through; it was typically travelled by school kids walking home, or in today's case, ruffians like us.

The next detail that I share is harder to look back on because I feel more than partially responsible for the way the situation played out from this point onward. It was trash day.

Why is trash day so important? On a normal day, this meant nothing more than the cans would be out, but today, I caught something that everybody had missed; there was a baseball bat inside a trash can.

I was walking behind my friends, and I tried to get their attention; I called out to them, but for some reason, they didn't pay me any attention. Maybe they were off in their own little world, maybe they genuinely didn't hear me, but as much as I frantically struggled to get their attention, they would not pay me any mind. I yelled to them, asking for help as the baseball bat was stuck in the trash can, and I couldn't get it out by myself. A deep feeling of despair overtook me as I came to the realization that the baseball bat had to have been placed there prior to our engagement; only a stupid person would assume this was mere coincidence. I felt like such a simpleton because in my repertoire of alternate realities, I did not consider the possibility that these gang-banging hoodlums may have brought a weapon.

I left the bat in the bin and caught up with my friends, informing them that there was a baseball bat in the garbage can. By that point, however, Rolando and his posse had turned the corner into The Alley. There was no getting it now.

I counted about ten people in our group, but there must have been at least twenty-two people on their end, some of which I'd never seen before, some of which I'm convinced didn't even go to our school, some of which, I swear were adults. I felt our collective hearts sink as we stood helplessly on the shore watching this tidal wave approach us. This was the second major development that I hadn't considered. Even with all of us, we were at very least outnumbered two-fold. We'd accounted for the possibility of being outnumbered, at least we thought. According to our fourteen-year-old math, between Elijah, Alfredo, Raven, Angel and I, we could take sixteen people (four each for Elijah and Angel, three each for Alfredo and Raven, and two for me). So, when our other friends got here, we should have been able to take on the world...

Speaking of all those people, none of them showed up...

Alfredo and Elijah both had criminal records of sorts; if they got in trouble again, they would face jail time. Apparently, there was a police car making its rounds around the route that kids walked home, which frightened off Alfredo and Elijah. I have no idea why the others didn't show up, but it was what it was.

Allow me to do the math and calculate how many people us four (thought) we could take. Four for Angel, three for Raven, two for me, and half a human for David... That was the penultimate nail in the coffin.

As their entourage approached ours, I was highly certain we were screwed. There was nothing we could have really done at that point except give our enemies the benefit of the doubt and hope that nothing bad would transpire. As they got closer, we noticed that they had the baseball bat with them.

As they approached, Raven and I mentioned the fact that they had the bat and berated them a little bit for having a weapon brought out. Gabriel gave the bat to one of his buddies and claimed they'd only use the bat "if somebody jumps in." We agreed, although with only four of us, it wasn't like we were in any position to make demands.

There was another piece of business that had to be taken care of. We needed people to look out and make sure nobody was coming. If the cops came (which happened from time to time), we needed someone to warn us. We agreed to have two people keep watch, one of our friends and one of their friends, each at different ends of the alley. Gay David volunteered to go and be the lookout; Raven and I were the only people available to help Angel if he needed it.

We formed a circle around where Angel and Rolando were going to fight. We stood on a barren patch of sand behind one of the houses. There were houses all throughout The Alley, but there were only backyards, and the tenets weren't typically found outside of their homes. On the other side of the circle, I saw people that I was friends with, which threw me for a loop. This one kid was named Joe, and he had been in fifth grade with me, Raven, and Angel. It was weird to see him on the other side, supporting someone who he had (presumably) less history with...

There were others that I knew around that semicircle also, supporting Rolando, but they were all affiliated with this street gang. In retrospect, poverty will really bring out the worst in kids. Thankfully, I was spared.

It was time for Angel and Rolando to get down to business and settle their beef once and for all. As kids flashed their cellphones to record, Angel took off his glasses and handed them to Raven.

Rolando took off his shirt, displaying a very skinny frame but otherwise not looking very intimidating. His excessively short hair made him look like all his hair had migrated to the top of his skull.

One kid was acting as the officiator and told them to commence the fighting. The two of them squared up with one another and needed little encouragement from the crowd. They both threw strikes at the exact same time. Angel threw a fierce uppercut that hit Rolando so hard I thought he knocked him out. Rolando's head jerked upward like a jack-in-the-box, and he fell to his knee. All it took was that one punch to convince me that Angel had won the fight. They could have quit right there, and I would have been satisfied. However, to Rolando's credit, he stood back up. The next thing I knew, Rolando was throwing a series of punches with some of them glancing across Angel's face, but none of them landing directly. Angel somehow managed to throw his arm across Rolando's head and get him in a headlock and then proceeded to punch Rolando's forehead about five times. Rolando had a cut above his eyebrow, and his mouth was bleeding. And then, they struggled a little bit more together until somehow, Angel ended up on the ground on top of Rolando. It was as if Angel did a half-assed judo hip toss that ended up in a dominant (albeit awkward) position.

Gabriel came forward, shouting at Angel, and kicked him in the face while he was on his knees. All Angel could do was cover up and protect himself. Gabriel shouted at Rolando to get up.

I couldn't believe what I was witnessing happening in front of me. I wanted to charge in and kick Gabriel in the head, but the kid with the bat brandished it.

After witnessing Gabriel jump in and kick my friend in the face to protect his friend, and after seeing the massive crowd that came with them, after seeing some strange faces of people who I am convinced had to have been adults, I came to realize that we weren't dealing with cowards... these weren't the typical sort of people we were used to dealing with. They were scumbags who protected their friends through any means necessary.

Gabriel backed up, and Angel rose to his feet again, bloodied from the kick to his nose. Rolando waited for him to square up again, which he did. Angel landed a few more shots before it was somehow taken to the ground again. Rolando was getting beaten badly, which prompted Gabriel to step in once again and commence the kicking.

I developed a raging hatred for this kid that I still hold to this day. I wanted to go in for the kill, to leap at him with everything that I had, if nothing else just to keep him off Angel. Unfortunately, the massive numbers behind him as well as the armed individual had me questioning whether I could do such a thing. They stopped me dead in my tracks.

He backed up once more, providing Angel the opportunity to stand up, but Angel backed away towards us. Rolando walked towards his friends as well.

Angel pleaded with us, "You guys," tears involuntarily flowed from his eyes, "if he does it again, I need you to help me."

To hear Angel in such desperation rallied all my courage. I was ready to charge them all head on regardless of their numbers and possession of a baseball bat. Angel and Rolando were going to engage again; however, adults had heard the commotion and were visibly concerned; they began snooping on us poor kids conducting our business. We all scattered and left the vicinity because we were certain the police were going to be called on us if they weren't already.

Following the confrontation, Raven, Angel and I walked to our friend's house, so Angel could wash himself up. He got himself cleaned up, and then we walked him home and everything else carried on as normal… I had a doctor's appointment that I had to go to immediately after, so my mom picked me up from Raven's house. As I rode towards the doctor, I saw Rolando and his friends walking towards a clinic.

Prior to leaving, we all agreed on two things: Gabriel was scum of the earth, and Angel had won the fight by a substantial margin.

That experience taught me a few things. The first thing it taught me was that there's always someone out there who is "badder" than you, which we all know by hearing it, but it's different when you witness it firsthand. While I had a knack for engaging in rough behavior, I had rarely encountered individuals who would fight the same way; and never had I encountered an individual who actually would jump in and fight on someone else's behalf. Seeing firsthand the engagement that took place between Angel and Rolando made me realize that we were way in over our heads; we were dealing with some bad apples. As troublesome as I may have been, I wasn't a bad kid, none of us were for that matter, but these guys pulled a weapon on us, probably brought their parents or uncles or whoever those adults were and threatened us with violence the likes of which are indiscriminately reserved for criminals. I was never fearful of people on a physical level, but I learned quickly to respect the willingness of others to fight in unique ways that favor them.

The second thing it convinced me of was that you cannot prepare for every little thing, which, again, I knew, but experiencing is different than hearing your elders tell you. There will always be a variable that you cannot determine, some possibility that you cannot see, or some consequences that you cannot predict. Assuming we had everything under control was a very bold thing to assume. It was very brazen and foolhardy for us to assume that we could handle every little thing that the world threw at us at such a young age.

I came to the realization that I needed to reflect on the way that I had been conducting myself up to that point. I believe there is value in being able to defend oneself and to possibly settle disputes with fisticuffs. I don't buy into the notion that every dispute can be settled through diplomacy; the people who believe that are short sighted. However, I also don't believe that everything can be solved through violence; the people who believe that are equally as short sighted. I think a balance exists between the two, and whether one favors either side heavily is one's own business. I can say in hindsight that we were fighting a battle that we shouldn't have been. Never mind the fact that we were dealing with bad people, we chose to engage in that behavior... we didn't just happen upon a band of misfits that came after us; we were willing participants.

I could have handled it if he lost the fight and got his ass kicked, but to be in a position where you watch someone get assaulted and you are powerless to stop it from happening is not a position I'd foreseen myself being in, nor is it one I would wish anyone to be in.

I felt guilty regarding the circumstances with the baseball bat; I still carry that guilt to this day. If I'd have taken the baseball bat, even just to throw it into somebody's yard where they wouldn't find it... that would have been helpful, but I left it there. Maybe if I'd taken up arms against them with the baseball bat, Gabriel wouldn't have interfered. Maybe he would have, and I would have cracked the side of his skull open; it's hard to say...

If you were to ask me if there's anything I would have done differently back then, I would say definitely. I'm not sure that I could have talked Angel out of fighting Rolando because he was a headstrong (stubborn) individual, but I could have intervened at the sight of trouble. Admittedly, I can't say with 100% certainty what would have happened, but I know I would have been a better friend had I stepped in and at least tried to help. For a long time, I felt like I was not a good friend to Angel because I left him there bleeding on the ground after a kid he wasn't even fighting kicked him in the face. I've never had this discussion with Angel, but I have had it with Raven. I've told Raven how I've regretted not being able to do anything, but it was a complicated situation. There's no perfect thing that anyone could have done in that situation, and you never really know what you're going to do in a certain situation until it happens. There's a saying that goes: "No plan survives contact with the enemy," and it proved true in our case... And back then, our plan didn't survive anything period. It just went up in flames.

Although I say I'd have done that differently, that's a momentary response. If I relived that situation again, that's what I'd wish I'd have done in the moment... but when I stop and think about the situation, I am reminded that there are unforeseen consequences that could have taken place. These kids, as I mentioned, were gang affiliated. If I took the baseball bat and just chucked it somewhere else where they couldn't find it, that may have given me the courage to defend my friend from harm, but I could have gotten jumped as well. Even if I mustered up the courage to go and defend my friend despite the fact that there was a baseball bat in the possession of an individual on the other side, I could have suffered brain damage or a broken bone, or a number of things. Furthermore, I could have gotten many people hurt in the process. So, if you ask me now, as a twenty-two-year-old man, if there's anything I would have done differently, I will tell you no. When considering the fact that this could have escalated the feud and created a prolonged conflict, we made out like bandits... all these years later, I'm beginning to realize this was a battle we were never going to win.

That does not change the fact that I still feel responsible for what happened, even after eight years. And in the long run, I know that I did the right thing, but it's not an easy thing to come to terms with. It doesn't soften the blow of what happened to my best friend, and it certainly doesn't soften the blows that he received, and it's not a conclusion that is easily reached. It's not as if you're picking out your favorite flavor of ice cream at the store; it is an intricate ocean of possibilities with an endless amount of potential consequences and repercussions that not even the most seasoned sailors could navigate through with certainty.

Still, even in admission of the fact that I did the right thing, that there was nothing better I could have done in the circumstances I was placed in, it does not make it easy to relive this experience. I think about it ever so often, at least once a month, because it was such a shitty thing to see happen at such a young age. I watched angrily as a young boy threatened me with a baseball bat. I watched hopelessly as my friend was assaulted with kicks to his face. I watched horrified as my friend curled into a ball like a wounded dog protecting his organs. I watched helplessly as my best friend's blood dried and smeared onto his face… I watched as my best friend's blood trickled down from his nose and splatted onto the hard, sunshine-colored sand.

I watched…

I'm sorry.

I'll never forget the sight of that sunshine-colored sand becoming crimson.

About the Author

Nathaniel Ritchey began his writing career at the age of seven when he began writing short stories inside his school notebooks. He continued to write short stories and began blogging when he turned sixteen. He made his professional debut in November of 2019 when his work titled "Love" appeared in Fairest Magazine®. He is currently working on his first novel and is also hoping to have an animated series developed in the near future. Nathaniel aspires to write because he considers himself a story-teller and will continue writing as long as he still has stories to tell. "For aspiring authors," he says, "find your voice; once you find that, I think everything else will fall into place."

Time is Dancing

Chloe Strickland

Lives of great men all remind us

We can make our lives sublime,

And, departing, leave behind us

Footprints on the sands of time;

Footprints, that perhaps another,

Sailing o'er life's solemn main,

A forlorn and shipwrecked brother,

Seeing, shall take heart again.

Henry Wadsworth Longfellow

Autumn had fallen into step with winter. The branches of the trees now shivered with frost, the pavement outside ached with ice, and the sun hid behind the clouds, denying the world below of its warmth.

Marla, buried under two sweaters and a scarf, shivered as she approached the building. As she stamped her shoes on the mat to get rid of the snow, she willed herself not to think of Fitz.

However, she could only think of Fitz. August Fitzgerald had successfully taken up all of the corners of Marla's mind.

Sleepy eyed, she squeezed herself onto the elevator with the other students; the slow drawl of the lift could have lulled her to sleep. The night before had been filled with tossing and turning and staring up at the ceiling with nothing but the rumbling of the heater to accompany her; all of her nights were like this now.

Sometimes, she wouldn't even bother trying to sleep. Instead, she would climb to the roof of her apartment building and look up at the stars. The vastness of the sky was both taunting and comforting. It was a reminder of how far Fitz was from her, that somewhere in time and space, he was travelling further and further away from her. But, it was also a comfort knowing that somewhere in time and space, they were still together.

The first time Marla met Fitz, she had been sitting in the quad of her university, enjoying the cool air and the blooming flowers in the trees, when he called out her name. His voice echoed around the buildings, and he rushed to her like he was reuniting with a lover after a war.

"I'm sorry," Marla squinted up at the gangly boy who stood above her. "I don't think we've met." Her hair, cut above her chin, fell from behind her ears as her eyes darted around at the other students who glared her way for disrupting their peace.

Not minding the stares he'd attracted, Fitz laughed from his belly, auburn hair falling in front of his eyes with the uncontained movement, "Of course we've met," he said, once he caught his breath from his laughing fit. "It just hasn't happened yet."

Fitz would later tell her that there were an infinite amount of universes where they did and didn't meet. That he preferred the ones where they did.

There was little to no explanation in the beginning; she chalked it up as Fitz's clever way to speak to her. Either way, they fell into friendship as easily as the bloomed flowers fell from their branches as summer creeped up on spring.

It had been months of coffee at midnight, stargazing until the sun came up, dancing to showtunes in the living room, and reading to each other in the morning sun.

The summer heat was merciless when Fitz told Marla that he could travel through time.

She lay on her belly flipping through her book; her hair stuck to the back of her neck and forehead with sweat dotted around her nose. Fitz was beside her on his side, propping himself up on his elbow and fiddling with the blanket beneath them. Marla resentfully tucked her hair behind her ear, complaining that it was at an awkward length and was inconvenient in the heat.

Fitz stared intently at the shadows of the leaves on Marla's back as he contemplated how to tell her. Then, he just blurted it out.

She didn't look up as she shook her head, hair brushing her shoulders, "Oh yeah, and where do you time-travel to?" she replied blandly.

Fitz frowned at her unamusement, letting his hands fall idle as he glared at Marla, "I'm serious."

Marla flipped a page of her book, "I am too. Where do you go?"

She only looked up when Fitz stayed silent. He had a pensive look on his face, brows pulled together in thought.

She chuckled, eyes crinkling at the corners, and rolled onto her back, holding her book above her head. "Fitz, I know I can be gullible sometimes, but it's just cruel of you to think I would believe that you're a time traveler."

"But, I am!" he insisted.

Rolling her eyes, Marla reached up and ruffled his russet hair. "It's not funny anymore."

With a heavy sigh, Fitz sat up, "What do you want? Proof?"

She had finally had enough of his game and sat up with him. "Yes, August, give me proof."

She expected him to break out in laughter, telling her that he had gotten her once again and they both would have moved onto another topic. She didn't expect to be in a different place in a millisecond when Fitz grabbed her hand.

Like a flash of lightning, Marla stood in the quad of her university, only, the sun didn't beat down on her. Instead, she felt a cool breeze against her skin and fan through her hair. The grassy area wasn't deserted due to the heat but rather was full of students, all lounging and enjoying the beautiful springtime.

Marla was stricken with waves of confusion and terror when a voice shouted through the quad, breaking through the peaceful quiet. "Marla!"

Her hair whipped against her cheeks as her head turned, following the call of her name. It was Fitz, running full speed across the grass. But it wasn't *her* Fitz. *Her* Fitz stood right next to her, still holding her hand.

This Fitz ran across the grass to a figure sitting under a tree- a figure that Marla quickly realized was her, with paler skin from the lack of sun and hair an inch shorter.

As the *other* Fitz stood before the *other* Marla, she realized what she was witnessing.

It was the day Marla met Fitz.

The two watched the meeting in silence, mostly because Marla was too awestruck to speak. When the *other* Fitz had taken a seat next to his new friend, Marla turned to *her* Fitz, eyes watery and speechless.

Fitz's rosy cheeks were sore from his grinning. "Do you believe me now?"

He revealed everything to her then; how he travelled aimlessly through time and, in his journey, mistakenly fell into a timeline where he met this gullible girl who loved the stars. How he couldn't find it in himself to leave after meeting her.

He told her about the universe, how there were parallel worlds and infinite possibilities for everything. "Everything that *can* happen, *will* happen. And not only *will* it happen, it *is* happening. And everything that *has* happened is *still* happening."

"Can't you cause damage by staying in a timeline that isn't yours?" she asked once when they were quietly reading over breakfast.

"I haven't caused any yet." He smiled cheekily.

It was a love of the soul. Marla loved August Fitzgerald like a brother. He'd brought her the heat of the sun and blooming flowers when her life was frozen in a permanent winter.

And Fitz, who'd lived a life of constantly travelling through the fabric of time, felt as though, for once, time was frozen. He wasn't from this timeline, but it felt like home to him. And he loved Marla more than he could understand it.

When Autumn came and the leaves started falling, so did pieces of time. Fitz noticed things going wrong; people losing time, forgetting things, and days repeating with no one noticing. No one but Fitz.

Worst of all, Fitz was forgetting things from his own life. He couldn't remember his father's name, if he had a brother or a sister, or what color his mother's eyes were.

"I'm disappearing from my own timeline," he explained to Marla. "And being here, I'm afraid I might disappear completely."

Marla was caught off guard. She just stared squarely at Fitz, trying to process what he was saying and what he might say next.

"I've never stayed somewhere this long," Fitz continued. "I'm forgetting things from my own life, and there are things going wrong here that you haven't noticed, but I have."

"You have to go back," she uttered, voice sounding defeated.

He held her hands in his, and he could feel them shake. "I am so sorry, Marla."

Marla wanted to be angry with him, to scream that he should never have gambled with time. Instead, he had fallen into her life, and she loved him so dearly, she couldn't bear the idea of losing him. But, she had to.

He vowed to return, that she would see him again, but they both knew things would never be the same, that time would never allow them to truly be together.

A year had gone by, but Fitz was always on her mind. She searched for him everywhere. She spun and looked in every direction when she felt the familiarity of deja vu, searching for his copper hair in a crowd. She would feel disoriented trying to figure out if she'd just spaced out or if she lost time, if there was a tear in the timeline and a certain gangly boy had wandered into her world. He never did, and Marla felt as though the sun would stay hidden behind the clouds and never return to her.

Marla stepped out of the elevator and, with the crowd of other students, made her way to her next lecture. Before taking her seat, she unwrapped her scarf, letting her hair fall to the middle of her back.

After reviewing the notes from the last lecture, she turned to a new page to start the new lesson, but found two more pages of notes in her handwriting that she had no recollection of taking. She stared muddledly at the content of the pages. When her professor began writing his lesson on the board, Marla was baffled to see that it was already written on these pages. Her heart began picking up pace.

With shaky breath, she leaned to the person next to her, "Is this review?"

"No, this is all new stuff."

Her heart sank. She gathered her papers and didn't bother shoving them back into her bag. Her footsteps echoed through the quiet lecture hall as she ran out of the building.

Once out the doors, she searched in every direction, minding none of the looks from the students passing by. She spun and scanned over the crowd of students, lifting onto her toes, searching for August Fitzgerald.

In her flurry, someone bumped her and knocked all of her papers out of her hand. Her breath was shaky and hands trembling when she knelt to pick everything up.

She sighed, surrendering and being let down once more. The papers had become wet from the frost on the pavement, and her notes were smudged, now indecipherable. Fingers now frost-bitten, she numbly gathered the stack of papers.

She sniffed and tried to hold back the tears that were threatening to spill over when tattered shoes that she recognized stepped into her view.

She looked up, squinted at the silvery sun shining from behind the clouds, and up at the gangly boy with auburn hair that stood before her.

She rose from her place on the ground, smudgy notes forgotten, and gazed at him in disbelief. She reached out, and he took her hand in his; she felt he could defrost her entire being. He was really there, her Fitz.

His ruddy cheeks were sore from grinning widely as he pulled her close, "Hello, Marla."

About the Author

Chloe Strickland is a student writer who has been writing since she was a child. Born and raised in the Coachella Valley, Strickland began writing stories recounting her daily life in the desert. As a teenager, she began writing poetry and expanded from the narrative genre to science fiction and fantasy. By the time she was twenty, Strickland would have written dozens of short stories and over two hundred poems. Having earned an associate degree in both English and journalism at College of the Desert, Strickland plans on continuing her education and hopes to work in publishing.

Sitting at home in her beautifully decorated dining room, Valerie is at the table with her attention trained on her laptop. Just as she decides to check her email, a new one comes in. Clicking it open, she sees it is from Gordon, her new 'friend' from the coffee shop that she had met just that morning.

"Valerie, what are you doing besides working on your laptop?" his email reads.

Valerie smiles, as she reads his assuming question. "How do you know I'm working? I could be doing something else."

"Look how fast you replied. Timing is everything," Gordon replies.

Valerie laughs at his response, as she types, "So, what's up, Gordon?"

While she awaits his next witty reply, she walks into the kitchen for a cup of coffee. Smelling the sweet yet strong aroma, she pours herself a cup and returns to her laptop, hoping to see another email from Gordon.

Gordon is at his home in the living room as well. Only he is at his coffee table, sipping a smooth glass of wine. Continuing their email banter, he writes, "I have a question for you."

Without hesitation, Valerie responds, "I'm listening," as she wonders where the conversation is going. Because she had just met him, she has no idea where his mind is or what his intentions are towards her. But, she is definitely interested in finding out. While Valerie is wondering about the handsome man on the other end of the computer connection, his question comes in.

"So, how is it that a beautiful woman like yourself is not married or involved with someone?"

Seeing where the conversation is headed, Valerie goes along with his direction. "I was involved with this guy for a couple of years until I found out that he met a female online. He left me for her. I haven't seen or heard from him since." Valerie didn't really want to go into the conversation, but she felt comfortable discussing it behind the shelter of the computer screen.

Her response peeked Gordon's curiosity, causing him to ask, "How long has it been since that happened?"

"Around five or six months now." Then, turning the focus away from her, she inquired about his romantic life, without waiting for his response to her last answer. "What about you? Why don't you have a special someone in your life?"

"I went through something similar. I was with a woman for close to a year; then, I found out she was cheating on me. I let her go because I didn't want to be with someone who wanted to be with me and someone else." Gordon began to reminisce about his past relationship, while looking out the window. Quickly, he decided to let it pass and look toward the future. So, he wrote, "Come off that computer. Let's go and have some fun."

Although she was amenable to the open conversation, she had not anticipated the invitation. "I just met you today. I don't know anything about you nor do you know anything about me." She was really unsure about his invitation. She didn't know what to make of it. She was accustomed to taking precautions when it came to dating. Interrupting her thoughts, another email came through.

"What would you like to know? Just ask, and I will tell you. I'm not trying to hurt you. I just want to get to know you better. Just want to have some fun for a change. Nothing serious just fun. So, how about it?"

As she reads his words, she wants to believe in their innocence, but she can't help to question his intentions. "So, where are you talking about going?"

Becoming hopeful at the prospect of seeing her again, he grins as he types, "It's a surprise."

✱✱✱

Having finally ended her work day, Diane is home relaxing in her family room. The pains she was experiencing earlier are continuing to annoy her. Trying to find a comfortable position, she lies down on the couch, then the recliner, next the sofa bed... To her dismay, she cannot find comfort anywhere. Finally, she walks into the master bedroom and into her well-used bathroom. Opening the medicine cabinet, she reaches for the Midol and quickly downs a couple of the pills.

As she waits for the Midol to kick in, she lies down on the bedroom floor with her legs uplifted on the bed. As time goes on, she drifts off to sleep only to be awakened by stabbing pains in her abdomen. So, back to the bathroom she goes to retrieve more pills. Suddenly, the lights go out!

"What the hell!" Diane exclaims. "This doesn't make no damn sense! How am I supposed to suffer in the dark? Let there be light!" Then, she thought to herself, *What am I doing? I'm not God.*

To help relieve the situation of being surrounded by darkness, she goes to the kitchen and retrieves a candle from the drawer and lights it. Returning to her room, she begins to pray, "Lord, I need help in a real way!" After placing the candle on her night table, she again lies on the floor, as she continues to pray. "Lord, I'm lying here in the dark in agony! Can you please send me a miracle? Or, at least can you please shorten this week? This is a hot mess! I need new furniture, a bed, a car, and most of all, I need light! In Jesus' name, I pray. Amen." Then, she opens her eyes.

As if though she is surprised to see the outcome of her prayer or the lack thereof, she yells, "Lord, I'm still in the dark! I just prayed to you! Can you help a sistah out? I know you're busy! But, the rest of the world has light!" Then, to see how far the devastation runs, she picks up the remote and attempts to turn on the television. When a picture fails to appear, she screams out, "I don't have no electricity! I'm 'bout to have a fit up in here!"

*******YOU HAVE JUST READ CHAPTERS 4 & 5 OF CRAMPS,
A NOVEL BY LA NOYCE TAYLOR.*******

*******TO READ THE COMPLETE NOVEL, YOU CAN PURCHASE A COPY AT
BARNESANDNOBLE.COM OR AMAZON.COM*******

CRAMPS is the serious yet comedic tale of five women who live through the pains and discomforts of their womanhood that rears its head once every month.

In the midst of it all, two strangers meet and a connection is made. Will the connection last or will life get in the way?

Another woman struggles with her hysterics and the challenges she faces in everyday life. Will the mood swings get the best of her or will she be able to manage through it all?

Three women find themselves in the tailspin of their lives. What will happen to the man who ensnared them?

Finally, one young lady is swept up into the challenges of womanhood unaware of what it all means.

How will the women manage their life challenges as they strive to find a healthy balance in the midst of their monthly CRAMPS?

La Noyce Taylor

CLF Publishing, LLC.
www.clfpublishing.org

La Noyce Taylor's books are available at:
www.creativemindsbookstore.com
www.amazon.com
www.barnesandnoble.com

ISBN 978-1-945102-47-9

90000

9 781945 102479

About the Author

La Noyce Taylor was born and raised in Los Angeles. Growing up as a little girl, she loved to be in plays and things of that nature. As a teenager, she enrolled in Drama class at her middle and high schools to continue her passion. As an adult, she tried out for stand-up comedy at her church and for a comic show. She also took a chance in a small business doing Open Mic Nights (Talent Shows). From there, she went on and made a commercial. Then, she wrote a movie script believing that her vision would also come to life. It has been a long journey for her, and now that she has arrived, there is no turning back.

From **Despair** to **Repair:** *Lord, Continue to Order Our Steps*

Michael Todd
and
Cheryl Ryan-Todd

"The steps of a good man are ordered by the LORD:

and he delighteth in his way."

Psalm 37:23

His Story - Chapter One: Life Away From Home

High school was an exciting time in my life. It brought many adventures as well as many challenges. In December 1972, when I was on winter break during my freshman year of high school, I met Teresa, a beautiful seventeen-year-old girl at the Hollywood Skating Rink, on Hollywood and Western, in Los Angeles. After watching her for a while, I invited her to couple skate, which was the last skate to the last song of the night. She said if I would walk her to the bus stop afterward, she would skate with me. I agreed to her request, and she consented to mine. Our skate was the beginning of a three-year relationship that I would have with her from the time I was fourteen to the time I was seventeen.

After winter break, when school resumed in January, Teresa was looking forward to completing her senior year, while I was still getting my sophomore year fully underway. But, things weren't going as smoothly as Teresa would have liked. She informed me she was ten credits short of graduating, and graduation was only six months away- in June. To ensure she graduated in a timely manner, I enrolled her into Jefferson High School's night program, and she attended classes on Tuesday and Thursday night. To guarantee she completed her classwork and homework, I attended classes with her although I was not enrolled. That June, my girlfriend graduated high school. But there was one thing that was different about her than the other girls: She was one month pregnant. The next year in February of 1974, she gave birth to our daughter Michelle Lakiesha Todd.

One month later, the three of us began living together and continued to do so until four months before I graduated high school, which was approximately a year and a half later. Teresa decided the relationship wasn't working for her, and she asked me to leave.

During the year and a half that Teresa and I lived together, my mother would constantly ask my brother Kenneth, who was one year older than I was, if I was at school. Daily, he assured her I was present. After Teresa and I broke up, I moved back home with my parents and finished the last four months of my senior year and graduated high school in June 1975.

After graduating high school, I incessantly looked for a job but was continuously unsuccessful. I needed to provide for my daughter as well as myself, so I saw no other alternative except to join the United States Marine Corps. At the same time, I was looking forward to serving my country. On December 27, 1975, I left to Concord, California for a three-year stent in the Corps. I started off as a grunt and worked my way up to military police officer.

During my time in the service, I was able to go home each weekend, provide for my daughter, and send $25 savings bonds home to her, which she was later able to use for college. The Marines changed my life. I went from being an immature, young boy to being a mature man. My ideas changed, my dreams were developed, and my life goals were expanded. Furthermore, I learned to develop a five and ten-year plan for my life. After three years of spending time in the Corps and maturing both mentally and physically, in 1978, I changed from active duty to reserves, which I engaged in for three years, from 1978 to 1981.

During that same time frame, not only did I love serving my country, but I also had a love for dancing. In September 1975, a new friend of mine connected me with the television show *Soul Train*. For one month, as part of a dance team, I danced on *Soul Train*. That was an exciting time for me, and I was able to meet some of the great African-American singers, such as Al Green, Patti LaBelle, the Spinners,

Minnie Rippleton, etc. The friend that connected me with *Soul Train* was Deborah Marie Jones. During our interaction, we began a relationship, and from our union, we conceived a son who we named Michael Todd, Jr. He was born in 1977. Our relationship lasted for six years after coming to an end for one of the strangest reasons known to man: Deborah wanted to have a relationship with my brother Morgan, and he felt the same way.

Unbeknownst to me, Morgan and Deborah had been secretly seeing each other when I would be away from home at work. At that time, I worked graveyard, and no sooner than I would leave my home, Morgan would come over. On some days, he would still be there when I arrived home. But, I thought nothing of it because Deborah would be doing his hair, of which I was aware. After some time though, their involvement was revealed to me by Deborah's sister Donna by way of a telephone call. After being apprised of the situation, I confronted the two of them about their entanglement. At first, they denied it. However, as I continued to press the issue, they finally admitted they had been sleeping together. To say the least, I was very hurt and felt betrayed by them both.

At their request, I moved out, and my brother moved in. I went through a period of depression after the break up with Deborah. The bout of depression lasted for five months, and during that time, my father took me to Canada to get my mind off the situation. It is my firm belief that time cures all wounds. I was completely devastated -not so much about the break up between Deborah and myself, but I actually felt as though I had lost my son- to another man- my brother, who had the audacity to tell me not to worry about Mike, Jr because he would take care of him.

One month later, Deborah and Morgan were married and moved to Hawaii, where my brother was being stationed, as he had just joined the Army. They remained in Hawaii for three and a half years. Afterward, Deborah and Morgan returned to the mainland. However, one year and a half later, Morgan went to jail on a drug charge and divorced Deborah while inside.

Meanwhile, once I had returned from my five-month trip, Deborah's sister Donna and I began a relationship, and I moved in with her and her aunt. From our four-year union, we had three children: Jason, Myesha, and Jonathan. Donna and I even attempted to get married in Las Vegas. But because she was under age at seventeen, it was a 'no go.' Her aunt, with whom we lived, told me she had guardianship over at Donna, and she consented to the marriage. However, when we went to the court, we found out her aunt did not actually have legal guardianship over Donna. Her father, who was still living, did. Therefore, the court denied our request. At the end of our four-year relationship, I left Donna and moved back home with my parents. Donna eventually left California, taking my three children with her, and moved back to New Orleans.

Sometime later, while living at my parents' home, I woke up one morning, looked outside, and saw Deborah sleeping in my father's truck, which was parked in the front yard. I woke up Morgan and told him Deborah was outside, and his only response was, "I'm done with her." Unfortunately, Deborah was strung out on drugs, and she had come to our home looking for some, while leaving our ten-year-old son alone at home. I promptly called a cab, placed Deborah in it, and sent her back home. About a week later, I put my son on a plane and sent him to Deborah's father, knowing that would be a safer environment for him. About a week after that, Deborah herself went back to New Orleans. To this day, neither of them has returned to California.

As time went on, I met a woman named Sandra, and she and I conceived a son together. However, at the time, she did not tell me he was my son. She always claimed he was the son of a drug dealer with whom she was involved. However, when my son was fourteen years old and the man who was supposedly his father had died, I saw them in a grocery store, and Sandra lifted her hand, pointed at me, and told my son, "Hey, there is your daddy." Since that time, I have attempted to foster a healthy relationship with my son, just as I have with all my children.

A Point to Ponder

As a young man, I engaged in one relationship after another from the time I passed through puberty. I was a young man in school, trying to earn an education. Although I graduated high school at the scheduled time and had done well with my studies, what did I have to offer a young woman when I was still relying upon my parents to provide guidance and a roof over my head?
~~~~~~~~~~

To all the young people who may be reading this book- Before you enter into a relationship with another person, trying to offer him/her a better life, make sure your life is together. When two people are complete as individuals and have a solid foundation, they will make a strong unit. Otherwise, it is easy for chaos and uncertainty to enter and cause further confusion.

I learned- once I was older- time is the best teacher because with experience comes lessons learned. Those lessons make you better prepared for life. As a youth, one should explore and learn him/herself before engaging in a life-changing relationship with someone else.

Her Story - Chapter One: Childhood Memories

On August 7, 1959, in the small town of Marysville, California, which is situated in the flatlands of an agricultural area, fifty miles north of Sacramento and thirty miles north of Grass Valley, with only a population of 10,000, I came into this beautiful world. I am the second of four daughters born to my mother. My sister Cynthia Marie, the oldest of the crew, was born two years before I was. A year after my arrival, my sister Catherine Diane made her appearance. Finally, our baby sister Angela Marie was born three years after Catherine. And although it may be a rarity for most sisters, I am fortunate to be very close to *all* my sisters.

My childhood and adolescent years were interesting and fun-filled, while at the same time being confusing and tumultuous. One of the things that made my childhood interesting and comparatively different from others was I had a careless and curious habit of always wanting to escape my environment. For example, when I was four years old, I was at the laundromat with my mother and one of her friends. They were heavily engaged in their conversation and paid me very little attention. Bored with the atmosphere and lack of attention, I decided I no longer wanted to grace the laundromat with my presence. So while my mother was otherwise distracted, I walked out the front door and began traversing the sidewalk.

A police officer, who was familiar with me and my antics, drove by, saw me, picked me up, put me in his car, and asked me where I was coming from and where I was going. I responded to his questions by saying I was at the laundromat with my mother, but I had left because she was drinking beer with a friend of hers, and I was headed elsewhere. The truth was she was drinking 'root beer,' but I had neglected the 'root' in front of the 'beer.' I was four years old and was probably unaware of the difference between the two. But due to my inaccurate description, when the police officer arrived at the laundromat, he gave my mother a serious tongue-lashing.

That episode was just one of the many occasions where I felt the need to escape. Escaping gave me a sense of hyper excitement, as I did not enjoy being confined to one locale at any given time. I had a free spirit, and I wanted my physical being to experience the same independence.

As my life continued, curveballs were thrown at me from one occasion to another, making my life feel like a rollercoaster ride. One occurrence was when I was five years old. What was intended to be a pleasant activity with my siblings turned out to be a very horrific and life-altering experience. At a park, one block from our home, we were swinging, climbing trees, and playing hide-and-seek, as we had done any other day at the park. We were having a wonderfully splendid time, as children should. But our joyous time would come to an end. On that particular day, Virgil, one of the park workers, was going around asking various children if they wanted to see something exciting in the pump house. The pump house was where the sprinkler and electrical system were housed. We had never been inside before, our curiosity led some of the children to tell Virgil yes, while others told him no- either from disinterest or fear of the unknown.

Finally, he decided to approach members of my family. First, he asked my sister Cathy if she wanted to see what was inside. She responded affirmatively, but once inside, she was very disturbed by what he attempted to do to her, and she ran out saying, "No, no, no." When he approached me, I completely ignored my sister's reaction and neglected to see it as a warning. I graciously accepted Virgil's invitation.

My 'beware of stranger danger' antennas were not operating effectively on that day. Slowly, I walked down the stairs into the pump house. Virgil requested I position myself against the wall once I was inside. I did as I was told. What he did next was unwelcomed and unexpected. He pulled down my pants and inserted two fingers into my vagina, causing me pain and horror. Right at that moment, Cathy came in and saw what was happening. Immediately, she ran to tell our oldest sister Cynthia and our mother.

Virgil grew frightened, and he attempted to flee the scene. However, his escape would prove futile. With her quick wit, Cynthia wrote down his license plate, and the authorities were summoned. Virgil was apprehended and was sentenced to eight years in jail for the crime he committed against me and as well as crimes he had committed against other children. While the outcome with Virgil was to be celebrated, there was another outcome involving the incident that only caused me more drama and feelings of anxiety. While I was in the pump house with Virgil, some of the neighborhood boys had also come in and saw what he was doing to me, and rather than feeling sympathy for me, they teased me about it incessantly. The teasing created feelings of sadness and remorse. I even felt alienated from the rest of my peers. To make matters worse, over time, the teasing increased, and my stepfather went to speak to the boys' parents, in an attempt to get the teasing to cease.

After the horrible incident with Virgil, my life eventually returned to "normal," and there was no more mention of it. At six and seven years of age, I loved to compose plays and coordinate singing contests in my neighborhood. I would design props and costumes and solicit neighbors' participation for the plays and singing contest. But of course, I was always the star of the show. That was a must. However, when I wasn't busy playing the lead role or trying to out sing my neighbors, my sister and I would sit on an inner tube and float down Feather River. Oh, what fun that was for us!

However, life was not always so peachy keen. At the age of nine years old, I suffered severe head trauma. A group of people was playing a game, and I thought it would be fun to join in. Despite my efforts to join the game, I was told to move out of their way. Being my usual stubborn and ornery self, I refused to abide by their request and found myself being hit in the head with a golf club. I felt my body vibrate in the vey spot I stood. A weird sensation ran through my body, and I found myself laughing uncontrollably. Strangely, I viewed the situation as hilarious- until I saw the blood running down the side of my face. Instantaneously, I realized the situation was serious. I had thought I could assert my will to be included in the game; however, I quickly learned I would not always be included in what others engaged in, and it was best to heed warnings when they came.

Another wonderful pastime I engaged in, from nine years old until I graduated high school, was playing sports. I loved to have play tetherball, baseball, basketball (even though I wasn't very good at it), and volleyball. My teachers encouraged me to participate in sports, believing the activities would help me to overcome my low self-esteem. They were absolutely correct. The sports allowed me to demonstrate my accomplishments and help me feel competent versus incompetent and incapable.

My low self-esteem may have been a result of my mother's abandonment of my sisters and me when I was twelve years old. (My father had made his exit long before, when I was three). After my mother chose to leave our home, my sisters and I were left to raise ourselves for the next six years. The feeling of abandonment left me feeling unwanted and insecure. Although she did not stay in the home with us any longer, she continued to be responsible for the household bills, and she brought us food on a weekly basis. Periodically, she would come and spend the night with us. I suppose she figured if she provided food, clothing, and shelter, her motherly responsibilities were covered. In addition to the physical needs we had, we needed love and guidance. Fortunately, our grandparents, who lived thirty miles away in Grass Valley, provided the guidance we needed. They played a pivotal role in our lives by teaching us manners and respect. Daily doses of love from a constant adult figure in our lives, however, was lacking. In later days, that void would begin to speak out and require fulfillment.

In addition to my mother leaving when I was twelve, my life took another turn. I began experimenting with oral sex. I believe that change in my behavior was due to not having a father figure to guide me and a mother who was intermittent in my life. A year later at thirteen years of age, physically I was very developed, and my sexual activities increased. I had my first sexual encounter with a boy who I had a major crush on. The experience only lasted five minutes- if that. I was greatly disappointed because I did not feel a thing, and I was left wondering, *This is the big step everyone is talking about?* The experience was very hum drum, and to make matters worse, the boy cared nothing for me while I thought he was the cat's meow.

To compound my state of engaging in underage sexual activity, I was also entangled with a group of teenagers of all races. One of our frequent activities was smoking marijuana while hiding from the cops who drove around our neighborhood. Although we smoked and could be easily considered a 'bad bunch,' we never got into any trouble or broke any laws- well, except for smoking marijuana- that is. The only thing I did was steal a Christmas light from someone's home. And unfortunately, I did get caught. Other than that, we pulled no mean stunts and played no tricks on anyone.

At age thirteen, when I was in junior high school, the plot of my life really began to thicken. I lent my marijuana pipe to one of my friends, and she got caught with it in her possession. While being interrogated by the authorities, she snitched on me, and the police promptly came to the school and arrested me. I was required to spend three days in juvenile hall. To exacerbate the influence of authorities in my life, my mother was called to the scene. She was required to retrieve me after my three-day stay. At that time, possession of marijuana was a felony, and the authorities wanted me to understand the seriousness of my offense.

While I was in juvenile hall, I shared a cell with a girl who was both psychologically and emotionally disturbed. She habitually cut her wrists with glass, which for her was a method of relieving the pain she felt. When the blood ran down her arm, it was as though the pain she felt inside was being released. But, in time, she always felt the need to release it again. I truly felt very sorrow for her. At the time, I felt sorrow for myself as well. Being in juvenile hall was a very scary and lonely experience. However, experiencing the three-day mini vacation did not cause me to discontinue smoking. Nor did it discourage me from using acid, which was another habit I had picked up along the way. Quite frankly, I enjoyed the acid trips, for they gave me an awesome feeling.

As you read the account of this portion of my life, it may sound as though I was on a downward spiral. Thankfully though, my time during my high school years wasn't all filled with drug abuse, hiding from the cops, being engaged in sexual escapades, or dealing with juvenile authorities. I did engage myself constructively, such as being involved in agricultural work. During that season of my life, I acquired a job picking rotten tomatoes in the fields and bins of walnuts, making five dollars for each bin. I was also an almond harvester, a peach picker, and a duck feather puller, for $.25 a duck.

Furthermore, in high school, there was a restaurant on my high school campus called The Lemon Tree. The restaurant was open to students, staff, and faculty. I was enrolled in a course similar to the modern home economics course and was able to work in the restaurant and learn a few skills. That particular job was a nonpaying job, as it offered credits for my high school diploma. So, continuing with my delinquent ways and striving to earn money, each day of high school from tenth grade to twelfth grade, I hid bags of marijuana in my socks and sold them to my peers. At the same time, I smoked marijuana myself, but I continued to go to school every day and earn A's and B's.

My attempts to earn money did not stop there. I did acquire a legal paying job during that same time frame and worked in the Marysville library during my junior and senior year of high school. I certainly had a good time there reading books to the young children and just being in that overall environment. My baby sister and her friends would come to the library to visit me as well, making my days even more enjoyable.

After working in the library during the daytime, our evenings at home were filled with even more excitement. Our house was known as the party house, as everyone knew there were no parents there. Our friends and their friends would come over with bottles of alcohol, and we would smoke and drink the nights away.

Throughout my teenage years, as I developed mentally, physically, and emotionally, to my discovery, I learned I had a bad temper. My bad temper was mirrored in my older sister, and together we had knock down – drag out fights with one another. We would hit each other's heads against the floor, knock holes in the walls, and kick the bathroom door down as we fought. Through it all, we loved one another; we just had an unexplainable aggression that erupted from time to time. Much of the anger and physical violence on my part was due to being a heavy drinker during that time. And because there were no adults in the house- no one to mediate our arguments and altercations- we would fight until tiredness overcame us and caused us to cease physically abusing one another.

Through all of the dysfunction, absence of my mother and a solid father-figure, guidance from my teachers and counselors, working legal and illegal jobs, dealing with an overactive libido, and engaging in physical violence, I did successfully graduate high school at the age of seventeen. And for that, I am proud!

A Point to Ponder

Just because a person grows up in an environment that lacks nurture and guidance does not mean the person cannot love herself enough to grow into a mentally and emotionally strong individual.

However, when the odds are stacked against her, she will have to use every positive avenue available to her to become the person God already predestined her to become.

*****YOU HAVE JUST READ CHAPTERS 1 & 1 of
FROM DESPAIR TO REPAIR,
A NOVEL BY MICHAEL AND CHERYL TODD*****

*****TO READ THE COMPLETE NOVEL, YOU CAN PURCHASE A COPY AT
BARNESANDNOBLE.COM OR AMAZON.COM*****

About the Authors

Michael Todd is a minister of the gospel of Jesus Christ. To prepare for his service as a minister, he attended the LPH Bible Institute while serving as both an usher and deacon.

Cheryl Ryan-Todd is currently retired, after suffering a slight disability.

Both are still active in their church and seek to serve the Lord within their full capabilities.

Michael and Cheryl Todd both lived through a childhood and young adulthood that was filled with experiences that sent them headfirst into one deeper challenge after another. They fought to keep their heads above water to refrain from drowning in their relationships, drug abuse, and family drama that taunted them.

Attempting to tread lightly, they found their footsteps were heavier than anticipated. Consequently, they ended up in scenarios they never imagined possible. But, there they were.

After having experienced the bitter pill only life on this side of glory could offer, they began to experience a longing desire for true happiness, joy, and peace. Cheryl had searched for joy and peace in men and marijuana, and Michael had tried marijuana and stronger drugs to achieve the sensations and feelings he desired. Neither was successful!

As God's favor was on their side, what Michael's and Cheryl's futures held would only come to pass if God Himself held an intervention.

CLF Publishing, LLC.
www.clfpublishing.org

Michael Todd and Cheryl Ryan-Todd's books are available at:
www.creativemindsbookstore.com
www.amazon.com
www.barnesandnoble.com

ISBN 978-1-945102-19-6

90000

9 781945 102196

Progress > Perfection

Janae Walker

"This highway leads to the shadowy tip of reality; you're on a through route to the land of the different, the bizarre, the unexplainable...go as far as you like on this road. Its limits are only those of mind itself. Ladies and gentlemen, you're entering the wondrous dimension of imagination... next stop, The Twilight Zone"

Rod Sterling

To live and to be alive. What is the difference? Zula had this thought in the back of her mind for the past nine months. As a senior in high school, it was her time to decide what path she was going to take. Every year, she was becoming more curious and eager to learn new things. As a child, she never dreamed about what she would be when she got older because her father always told her she would take over the family business in the bread factory. Coming from a poor background, she always assumed that she could not afford college. But in the year 3000, almost every available occupation requires a college diploma. Zula had the option of going to college and trying to pull her family out of debt or just working at the bread factory with her father. It was easier for her to stay within the family business doing a job she already knows how to do. Why take any risks or waste any money going to college when she already has a job set up for her? She loved growing up in San Francisco but knew that it was not meant to be her forever home. These are the thoughts recurring in her mind since college application season is just around the corner.

After spending many long nights thinking, Zula finally decided to start applying to colleges. Zula wondered if her own dreams should come first or should job security and survival come first. It was hard for her to not think about failing. Maybe she would go to college and then not be able to find a job after she graduates, or maybe college just isn't her thing and she wouldn't do well in her classes. This overthinking made it really hard for her to take any risks. But Zula was unhappy with the way she was living and knew something needed to change.

Two months later, Zula received a letter from the top school of her choice. She knew this moment would drastically change the way she spent her next four years. Slowly tearing the envelope open, she could hardly bear to look at what the letter could say. Again, her thoughts were taking over her mind. Twenty minutes later, she finally opened the letter. Inside, she found her acceptance letter. In that moment, she felt that her worrying all the time wasn't doing her any good. A lightbulb turned on in her head, telling her to do what she wants and live every moment like it is her last. She could ease her mind knowing that she is capable of doing things, and she knew exactly how the next four years of her life would go. She was looking forward to going to class, making new friends and going to college parties because that's what you would expect to happen during college, right? Sadly, none of this was true for Zula.

One month later, Zula graduated high school and was on her way to college. She had very little money in her pocket because her dad did not support her decision to go to college. But this did not concern Zula; she knew she would have the best experience of her life and a job when she completed college.

On the first day of school, Zula decided she was going to join a sorority called Chi Beta Thai. The sorority was designed to create lifelong friendships and volunteering in the community. To Zula, that sounded like the perfect opportunity to get involved at her new school, which it is supposed to be, until she attended the first meeting the next day. That decision changed her life forever.

After meeting a few people in the sorority, the orientation leader began to discuss the initiation process to get into the sorority, and that was when things started to get weird. Zula was told she needed to be readily available at any given time during the next ninety days. They also told her she could not tell anyone she was going through the hazing process until after it had been completed. None of the other girls in the room seemed surprised by that information, so Zula just went along with it.

The next morning at 3am, Zula received a call. She picked up the phone and heard a man's voice that she had never heard before. The man explained to her that she must pack a bag and be ready to leave campus by 4:30am. Assuming that was a part of the sorority initiation, she asked no questions and immediately got ready to leave. By 3:45, she was ready to go and headed outside to look for her ride. At exactly 4:30, a van approached her, and in the driver seat, there was a man. She assumed that had to be the man she had spoken to on the phone. She quickly hopped in the van, slightly suspicious as to what was going to happen and where they were going.

After one hour of driving down the highway, Zula finally worked up the courage to start asking the man some questions. When she asked where they were headed, he reminded her of the protocol for hazing rituals "no questions asked." Soon after, they arrived at a cabin next to a lake. It was a very secluded location with no other people in sight and no other cars driving by. The cabin looked empty and dark as if no one else was inside. The man told her to come inside, so that they can talk about her new home. "Home?" she wondered. At that moment Zula knew something was terribly wrong. As they walked into the house, Zula could only think that this entire situation was some sort of joke. She was supposed to be having fun doing team building activities and trying new things. Being held hostage was not something she could have ever predicted.

The man quickly rushed Zula up the steps and opened up the door to the cabin. The only visible thing was the furniture covered in plastic. It was a very large two-story cabin with many, many doors. Zula wondered if anyone else could possibly be living in the cabin. The man turned on a lamp and instructed her to have a seat at the table in the kitchen. The table looked very dirty and old as if it had not been touched in years. He knew his way around the house very well, so he had definitely been there before. After tidying up a bit, the man proceeded to introduce himself. He said, "Hi, I am not going to tell you my real name, but you can call me Mister. You are here because I chose you to be a part of my family." All Zula could do was cry. She was crying out of confusion and disbelief that that was her new reality. Once she calmed down, Mister went on to tell her that he had been keeping his eye on her for many years. He had been watching her all along to figure out everything about her but most importantly the way she thinks. Mister found it distressingly terrible that Zula was becoming this person who does not think about her decisions and the consequences in their life. He was being very protective as if he was her father or older brother.

Later on, Mister fell asleep. He seemed like he was in a deep sleep, so Zula took this opportunity to figure out their location and who Mister really was. There was no phone in sight, no television, and no computer. Zula wondered if anyone would even notice that she was gone. She kept her hopes up and continued to search for anything useful. All of the rooms were neatly organized, as if the cabin was set up to become a hotel. Seeing this made her even more afraid because she did not know exactly what his plans were. After an hour of searching, Zula had gone through twelve rooms and did not find anything useful. The only thing she could find were some very peculiar drawings. Each of the drawings were of different men and women. She did not recognize any of the people and just assumed they were fictional characters he made up for fun. But in the thirteenth room, she found a drawing of herself. This drawing was a very pleasant picture of Zula working at the bread factory. It finally hit her that for all these years she had a stalker, and she didn't even know what his real name was.

Once she found the pictures, she knew that there had to be more pieces to the puzzle. But Zula was exhausted, so she decided to have a seat on the staircase to catch her breath. She looked through the stair rails, staring at the terrifying cabin in the middle of nowhere. But in her head, she wondered, *If I am being held hostage, why am I not tied up? Why is he making it so easy for me to go through all his things? Why isn't he concerned that I could kill him in his sleep?* Then, she noticed right next to the chair Mister was sleeping in there was a file cabinet. She slowly stood up and walked down the stairs towards the file cabinet. It was now around 8:30am, and the sun was almost fully risen. Zula was scared she might wake him, but she knew if she wanted answers, she had to open it. She crept past him and very slowly began to slide open the top drawer of the file cabinet. Inside, she discovered one single file. The file had the name Russel Fredrickson written on it. Inside the file, there was a very thick packet, and on the front page, the words "CLIENT INFORMATION CONFIDENTIAL" were stamped on in bright red ink. Zula then realized this packet was from a therapist's office. The second page said that this patient, Russel, had Dissociative Identity Disorder. The therapist documented that Russel lost his family in a boating accident on a lake. A lake that just happened to have a cabin next to it that was owned by the Fredrickson family. Losing his family is what caused his mental illness. At that moment, everything began to make sense.

Zula began to put together all the pieces of the puzzle. The man who had been stalking her for many years had been studying her in an attempt to steal her personality. The pictures in the rooms are other people he had been obsessing over in order to add a larger presence of personalities in his own head. Zula knew that was the family he wanted her to be a part of, the family in his own head. In the second drawer of the file cabinet, she found many different files of other men and women of all different ages and races. The files were not medical files; they were his own personal files that documented each person's history and characteristics. But one piece of the puzzle didn't fit yet. Zula could not figure out why Russel brought her to the cabin instead of continuing to study her personality from a distance. Before she tried to escape, she just wanted to get answers. She did not understand why she was chosen over all the other people that were being watched.

Russel began to wake, so Zula quickly put away the files and pretended to be asleep on the couch. She laid there with her eyes closed and could hear Russel run up the stairs quickly into a room and shut the door behind him. Shortly after, she heard some very peculiar, childlike noises coming from the room. He was changing into one of his other personalities. Zula opened the file cabinet to quickly find out the name of the youngest child's personality he had stolen. The youngest child she could find was a girl named Susana. Susana's file said she loved to play dress up and tell stories with her friends. Zula planned to speak to the child and try to trigger Russel's personality to come out so she could speak to him.

She walked up the stairs and asked Susana if she wanted to come out of the room to read a new story. Susana came out of the room in a princess outfit and ready to read a new story. Zula began telling a story about a happy family who loved to spend time together. Zula described all the things you would expect to happen in a happy family but then tragedy struck. Everyone in the family was killed during a Tsunami on their vacation. The tragic story instantly made Susana run into a different room and slam the door behind her. Zula sat and waited for the right time to approach the room door. After about five minutes of sitting, she heard nothing from the room, and she was starting to worry. But then, the door started to creep open and based on the sinister grin he had, she could immediately tell that Russel was back.

Zula was confident she could get the answers she wanted because she knew exactly who she was dealing with. As he walked down the stairs, he greeted Zula and asked her what she wanted to eat. She declined the food offer and asked him to come have a seat, so they could discuss their family. She knew she had to be extra careful and try not to say anything that might trigger another personality to come out. Zula started off by trying to have small talk with him and asked him questions about how he originally saw her. Since she called herself a part of the family, which made him believe that they had a bond, he told Zula everything.

He started to watch Zula at the very beginning of her freshman year of high school, around four years ago. She was chosen by him because he liked how she always made the right decision. It reminded him of himself when he was in high school. But Russel was upset when Zula started to change her usual pattern of taking the safe route. She could've stayed with her father forever and never have to take risks out in the world. But she was going to college and joining sororities and leaving her father. Russel believed her actions were wrong and that she needed to be shown what can happen when you take risks. It was the perfect opportunity for him to come and take her when she tried to do something out of the usual. He did not understand why she would ever make those decisions. Out of all the stolen personalities Russel had, he couldn't understand Zula's personality from a distance, so he had to take her.

After hearing that, Zula finally knew the answer to the question she had been asking herself for the past year now: What does it mean to live and to be alive? So, she explained it to Russel because she knew it would help him understand why she changed. "Living is easy. You breathe in and you breathe out... You do what everyone expects you to do and sustain your life by doing the bare minimum, but being alive is not about preserving your breaths. It's about forgetting to breathe by finding passion and making your own path. It's being fearless and doing what you want to do." Russel was shocked hearing this. It seemed as if a lightbulb turned on in his head, telling him it is okay to experience stress and failure in life. As they both had a moment of realization, they sat in silence.

Zula broke the silence by offering to help Russel get back into therapy. Russel felt like he needed to become independent in order to properly grieve his family, so he agreed. It was an eye-opening experience for both of them. By noon, Russel and Zula were back in the van headed back to the college. She was not afraid of him anymore and promised him she would do everything in her power to make sure he gets well and finds people he can call family. Difficult roads really can lead to beautiful destinations.

About the Author

Janae Walker is a college student who is always looking to try new things. She is working towards her Bachelor's degree and hopes she will accomplish great things both during and after college. Some of her favorite foods are hot wings and enchiladas. In her free time, she likes to do research and read articles on various topics. Stories with lots of mystery and drama pique her interests the most. She also enjoys traveling and plans to travel more in the future.

From the Valley to Victory

Audrey Pearl Williams

"Yea, though I walk through the valley of the shadow of death, I will fear no evil; For You are with me; Your rod and Your staff, they comfort me."

Psalm 23:4 NKJV

Valley Life

Children are born all times of the year and under different circumstances. Some in cold weather, while others in warm, sunny or hot weather. Some to single mothers or to happily married couples. For me, Audrey Pearl, well I was born during the very hot summer of August 1943 on the 27th day, in Merced, California. For my wonderful parents Troy and Ella Bradford, I was their fifth child. My stay in Merced, however, would prove to be brief because soon after my birth, my family and I moved to Madera, California. The exact time frame the move took place I'm not quite sure. I was a bit too young to remember. However, I do know we moved to a three-room house at 324 Hull Street. Our home consisted of a bedroom, a living room, and a kitchen. Even though there were quite a few people living in the three-room house, it was just fine for me. I had a normal and happy childhood.

My father, who worked construction, was the breadwinner of the family. As a result of his hard work and commitment to providing for his family, I always had lunch money, school clothes, a roof over my head, and food in my stomach. At five years old, I started school and attended kindergarten at Persia Elementary school. That was an exciting time in my life.

And, just like any other child, I got into my share of mischief. I remember eating mulberries from the trees, even when I was forbidden by my mother. The mulberries colored my mouth and would give me away each and every time. My mother would question me about my activity, and I would deny it. But, of course, she knew better.

After attending Persia Elementary for about a year, Sierra Vista Elementary School was built, and all of the children were transferred over because Persia was being torn down. Sierra Vista was further away from home, and we had to cross a field to get to it, but it was a new school, and all the students, including me, were ecstatic.

By the third grade, I had grown very comfortable with being in a school environment, so I began to increase my activities outside the classroom. I decided to expand my horizons, by gaining a job in the school cafeteria. I enjoyed my job immensely, and it gave me a sense of responsibility, which made me very proud. During that same time frame, I remember getting a new Schwinn bicycle. I was the only one in the neighborhood who had one, so I felt extra special and even more proud. Each afternoon after school, I rode my beautiful bike up and down the street, grinning and laughing all the way. My father was the one who bought the bike for me, and I loved it that much more because he did.

Growing up, I spent a lot of time with my father. I remember sitting on his leg, outside on the porch, listening to him tell stories. I also enjoyed riding in his T-Model Ford, which I fondly called "the tick-i-licker." The bond I shared with my father was unbreakable.

While my father took the responsibility of providing financially for the family, my mother took responsibility for our spiritual well-being. To ensure we were spiritually grounded, she took us to church on a regular basis, so we could develop a relationship with our heavenly father. We attended union meetings by way of the bus and Sunday worship service and Sunday school on a weekly basis.

At our church, we would often have revivals that would last for two weeks. I witnessed the power of God move in the place as miracles flowed throughout the building. People came in drunk but left out sober, and the sick were healed of various diseases. All of that took place in our little old-fashioned country church that was fully equipped with a heater in the back. Near the heater is where the women sat and fed their babies, keeping them comfortable and quiet, while Elder Wynn, our pastor, delivered the sermon. He was a dynamic speaker. As the miracles continued to move about, the members were slain in the spirit, and many spoke in tongues.

The revivals were not the only highlight of our church. For me, Sunday school was intriguing. I thoroughly enjoyed attending Sunday school with Mother Chapman. She taught me all about Jesus through a unique way of teaching Sunday school, which was with Sunday school cards instead of books like they use today. Each Sunday, the other children and I would go into our class, and Mother Chapman would give us a new Sunday school card. We were required to learn the Bible verse, so we could recite it the next Sunday.

Church was rather calm and attending on a weekly basis was a way of life for my siblings and me. However, as it has been said, "Expect the unexpected." At that time though, I did not know what was meant by the unexpected. But, soon I would quickly learn.

During one of the union meetings, when I was eight years old, a preacher spoke on the topic "Hell Fire." His message certainly grabbed and held my attention, to say the least. Right then and there, I decided hellfire was not something I wanted to ever endure. So at that moment, although I had been going to church for as long as I could remember, I decided to live for the Lord. After service, we went home, and I prepared for bed as usual. Not long after falling asleep, I had a nightmare that I still remember to this day. In the dream, flames leaped all around my body. I could literally feel the heat from them. The dream scared me to no end. It only confirmed the decision I had made just hours earlier: *Hellfire was not for me.*

By the time fifth grade rolled around, I was excelling in my studies, and I was even voted president of the student council. Not only was I academically inclined, but I also loved to engage in sports and other extracurricular activities. I played in tetherball tournaments, participated in talent shows, and learned to square dance. As a youth, I was a robust girl, but a few teachers made a few alterations to some items of clothing for me, so I could have suitable attire for the talent shows. They were a lot of fun, and I enjoyed them immensely.

During that time in my life (my elementary years), my relationship with my father was wonderful, and my interactions with my teachers and those in the community were favorable. However, I felt a change come about in the way my mother responded to me. She knew I loved my father unconditionally and that we had a bond that was unbreakable. However, there was a rift between my mother and father, and because of their disagreements, she didn't care for the affection I showed toward him. Her actions showed me on several occasions how dissatisfied she was with the love I openly displayed for my father.

Once when I was nine years old, I was playing with a neighborhood girl, and during the course of our playtime, the girl yelled out, "Audrey Pearl, you should not have done that!" Upon the girl's outburst, my mother came out, grabbed me by my hair, dragged me inside, and beat me, not bothering to ask what had occurred. To me, it seemed as though she took every opportunity she could to severely discipline me. Actually, she was taking the frustrations she had with my father out on me.

After some time, I grew very tired of the beatings, so one day, I opened the window and stuck my head out. My mother saw me and asked what I was doing, in a tone that demonstrated her disapproval. I replied, "Getting some air," as I inhaled and exhaled. For once, she ignored me and walked away.

By the time I had made it to the six grade, I was yet involved in community events and stage plays. At twelve years old, I was very aware of my surroundings, and I still believed I was living a good life. At the same time though, I started to reflect on my future and what types of occupations I would be able to engage in once I graduated high school. I had noticed the only occupations available in my town involved field work, and I knew that was definitely not for me.

Once I entered Thomas Jefferson Middle School, I really took an interest in history, which led me to reading a lot of history books and writing book reports. I continued along with my extracurricular activities and excelled in volleyball. I even enjoyed singing and even appeared on a television show to sing. However, I did not make the choir that year, and I was not involved in any talent shows.

As my mind both wandered and wondered, I once again took notice of the occupations that were available for me in my town and seriously considered how my life would be after high school and where I would live. I desired to have a career, and I wanted to see the world. But the question was, "How would I get out there to see it?" Eventually, I came up with the perfect answer. I was going to join the service, and inadvertently, I would see the world. Furthermore, I would have no children, and I would not marry. That became my decision and motivation for my future.

When I shared my brilliant idea with my mother, she looked at me and did not say a word. At that moment, I did not understand what her silence meant. I would later learn that she figured if I did not want to have children or get married and on top of it all join the service, I was probably a lesbian. So, she quickly devised other plans for me. It was always her desire for me to marry and have children.

To move her plan into motion, somewhere along the way, she chose Clarence, a friend of the family, to be my husband. He was seven years older than I was, and he was in the Navy. To ensure that Clarence and I would make a connection, she did not allow me to hang out or converse with other boys. However, when Clarence was home from the Navy, he was permitted to come to my house, and I could sit and speak with him and even go out on dates. He started to bring gifts for me when he would come by, which made my father furious, but he had lost his voice of authority in the house because of his extramarital activities. So, my fate was left in my mother's hands.

Not too long after I started dating Clarence, I became pregnant. There was a lot of talk throughout the town about my condition because I was a single young woman who would soon be a mother. Some were saying I was just a fast girl, while others were saying it was a case of statutory rape. To clear up the matter, my mother convinced a judge to allow Clarence and me to get married, but my father did not agree. He wanted me to give birth to the baby, then give the baby to my parents to raise, so I could continue with school. But that was not my mother's plan. She wanted me married, and that was the end of it. And, in an effort to continue to keep other guys away from me, she forced me to wear maternity clothes from the moment she learned I was pregnant even though I was not showing yet.

In June 1957, Clarence's father married us in his home. After the wedding, Clarence and I moved to San Francisco. At that moment, I reflected on my life and realized there I was pregnant and married, with no education. I felt completely in despair. And in the back of my mind, I remembered the dream of hellfire I had some years back. I wondered what would become of me.

Lessons Learned

At a young age, I learned very quickly that facts always override fantasy. Therefore, I had to face the new responsibilities that had developed in my life. As a result, I chose marriage versus being single and having a baby out of wedlock. For me, that was the best choice.

A Question to Ponder

Revisit your childhood momentarily, allowing your mind to recall times you spent with your family, at school, and during social, spiritual, and extracurricular activities. Which events helped to shape the person you are today? Which people greatly influenced your life- positively or negatively- and why? Were there any decisions made on your behalf with which you do/did not agree? What were they and how did they impact your life?

*******YOU HAVE JUST READ CHAPTER 1 of
FROM THE VALLEY TO VICTORY, A NOVEL BY AUDREY WILLIAMS*******

*******TO READ THE COMPLETE NOVEL, YOU CAN PURCHASE A COPY AT
BARNESANDNOBLE.COM OR AMAZON.COM*******

*T*he journey called life has many twists, turns, and uphill battles. Circumstances can catch a person unaware, leading him/her into an abyss of the unexpected. But, the Bible says, *"We are not ignorant of Satan's devices,"* (II Corinthians 2:11). Therefore, we do not have to fall prey to our adversary. Furthermore, with the Lord guiding us, we can make it through any circumstance, regardless of how tumultuous it may be.

Audrey Pearl Williams, from the age of thirteen, began to experience a life that was not the life she had planned or envisioned for herself. She had planned to graduate high school and then set out into the world, seeing all God had created for her to enjoy. But, almost in an instant, she found herself married and with child. Then, when she least expected it, her life grew increasingly disparaging, as she suffered through church ridicule and mean-spirited churchgoers, while she attempted to answer the call God had placed upon her life.

What became of Audrey after navigating through life's unexpected twists and turns, heartbreak and pains, unfulfilled dreams and losses? Did she eventually gain joy, fulfillment, and peace? Did God finally answer her prayers?

As you read this true story of Audrey Pearl's life, revisit your own life's journey and recall the power of God. Remember, He said in His Word, *"I will never leave you nor forsake you,"* (Hebrews 13:5). As Audrey traversed through her life's journey, God was with her every step of the way.

CLF Publishing, LLC.
www.clfpublishing.org

Audrey Pearl Williams' books are available at:
www.creativemindsbookstore.com
www.amazon.com
www.barnesandnoble.com

ISBN 978-1-945102-18-9

About the Editor

Dr. Cassundra White-Elliott resides in California with her family, where as an English/Education professor she works for various community colleges and universities.

When writing, she writes with the direction of the Holy Spirit, in an effort to share with God's people all that He has for them.

In addition to teaching and writing, Dr. White-Elliott also serves as an evangelistic teacher. She is also the founder of International Women's Commission, a ministry that serves the needs of the entire person, by attending to healing the mind, body, soul, and spirit.

Dr. White-Elliott holds a Ph.D. in Education, a Master's in English Composition, and a Bachelor's in Education.

Dr. White-Elliott is also the founder of CLF Publishing, LLC. For your publishing needs, go online to www.clfpublishing.org.